THE FARRINGTON FORTUNE

Whilst heading to London to visit her wealthy Godmother, Patricia is involved in a carriage accident that throws her into the path of Mr. Darvill, a very eligible 'parti'. After overhearing a derogatory comment about her opportune invasion of his privacy, Patricia wilfully declares herself to be a much sought after heiress who is seeking to escape from her many would-be suitors, little realising the consequences of her piqued response.

KAREN ABBOTT

THE FARRINGTON FORTUNE

Complete and Unabridged

LINFORD
Leicester

First published in Great Britain in 2009

First Linford Edition
published 2010

British Library CIP Data

Abbott, Karen.
 The Farrington fortune.- -
 (Linford romance library)
 1. Love stories.
 2. Large type books.
 I. Title II. Series
 823.9′2–dc22

 ISBN 978–1–44480–070–8

Published by
F. A. Thorpe (Publishing)
Anstey, Leicestershire

Set by Words & Graphics Ltd.
Anstey, Leicestershire
Printed and bound in Great Britain by
T. J. International Ltd., Padstow, Cornwall

This book is printed on acid-free paper

1

'Tricia! Tricia! You're going! You're really going!' Patricia Farrington's sister, Emily, younger than her by only twelve months, burst into the parlour of the country vicarage where her two sisters and their two brothers were engaged in their various pursuits on this cold wintry afternoon. Emily's face was alight with excitement as she anticipated the stir her announcement would cause. She wasn't disappointed.

Her brothers and sisters immediately looked up and all colour drained away from Patricia's face as she rose from the sofa, not noticing that the pillowslip on to which was doing some drawn thread work now lay at her feet on the faded carpet.

'Are you sure? How do you know? What have you heard?' She looked earnestly at her sister, her hands clasped at her breast. 'Is it indeed true?

You aren't humming me, are you? For that would be more than I could bear!'

'As if I would, Tricia dear! No, I overheard Mama telling Papa. It was in the letter . . . you know, the one Tomkins brought up from the village this morning. It was indeed from London . . . franked by some earl or other.'

'And from my Godmother?' Patricia asked urgently.

'Of course! Didn't I say?'

'No, but it does not matter. Do go on!'

'Well, I heard her say to Papa that you really must be allowed to go and Papa said to give him the letter and he would see for himself what Lady Hartridge had to say.'

'And?'

Emily's face fell slightly as she admitted, 'Well, I don't know any further because I realised that Mama was coming towards the door and I fled before she could catch me eavesdropping!'

'What do you think Papa will say? Do you think he will let me go?'

'I hope so!' Emily uttered, a rapt expression now lighting her pretty face. 'For then you may meet a handsome lord or some other sort of wealthy man who will fall in love with you and ask you to marry him . . . and then you can invite me to stay with you and I will take London by storm next season and make the most advantageous match!'

'And he will buy a commission for Thomas in the Hussars!' Patricia continued, her dark eyes sparkling.

'I should like that!' twenty-year-old Thomas declared with enthusiasm, turning away from the tall, glass-fronted cabinet which he was using as a looking glass as he attempted to fashion his necktie in a fall of elaborate folds.

'It costs about eight hundred pounds to buy a commission, you know . . . and I don't expect Papa could manage to find so much money.' He sighed, adding, 'Which is why he wants to launch me into politics, but I would much rather join a regiment in the army.'

'And what about Richard and me?' their younger sister, Meg, asked petulantly from where she was curled on the carpet near the fire playing with her doll. 'What will you do for us?'

'You will both have a promising future with none of the uncertainties that we have suffered,' Patricia assured her lightly, only momentarily distracted from Emily's announcement.

'Well, I think going to London sounds boring,' Richard piped up from the opposite side of the fireplace where he was busily whittling a piece of wood into the shape of an owl.

'Why, no!' Patricia cried. 'There will be balls and routs; visits to the theatre; concerts; picnics and assemblies! All kinds of things!'

'I bet she has written to say that she cannot invite you!' Richard retorted.

'Don't be horrid!' Emily rounded upon him. 'If it were to refuse Patricia's visit, why did Mama take the letter to

Papa in his study when he is preparing for his Sunday sermon? No, I regard the matter as settled already. Patricia is going to London for the Season.'

This hopeful pronouncement proved to be well founded and, not only that, but Lady Hartridge had added that she would take great pleasure in presenting her Goddaughter at one of the drawing-rooms.

Needless to say, the homely vicarage became the scene of a flurry of dressmaking over the next few weeks. This needed some ingenuity for, although the living of Haxley was respectable, it being worth some three hundred pounds a year, Patricia knew that the day-by-day claims of a large family of five growing children left little to be spent on the extras of life.

Harriet Farrington led her two elder daughters upstairs and into her dressing room, where her maid had arranged the contents of a large travelling trunk over the various pieces of furniture, making a bright array of gowns and accessories.

Patricia and Emily looked at their mother with puzzled eyes.

'These were my gowns when I was about your age,' Harriet explained, smiling at their bewilderment. She had been born into a genteel family who lived on the fringe of the elite of local society and was regarded as having married beneath her expectations when her heart's choice fell upon the younger son of a landed gentleman, whose chosen career was in the church.

Now, she hoped to improve the chances of her daughters making eligible matches by enabling Patricia to have the opportunity to shine further afield than their neighbouring town of Southport. It was an added bonus that her schooldays' friend, Lady Hartridge, had but one son . . . and no daughters of her own to launch into society — for they would undoubtedly have taken precedence over the strongest of girl-hood pledges.

Harriet sighed with the sheerest pleasure as she recalled her friend's enthusiastic response to her request that maybe she would consider chaperoning Patricia to a series of balls, routs and assemblies during the following Season. Indeed, Lady Hartridge wrote that she would thoroughly enjoy the experience, especially as life was excessively dull at the moment since her only son had taken himself travelling on the continent and, although Mrs Farrington had not actually mentioned her main aim in sending her eldest daughter for a Season in London, Lady Hartridge assured her friend that she would leave no stone unturned in securing a suitable husband and, indeed, already had several eligible parties in mind.

Patricia's face fell as gown after gown was lifted for their inspection. Her generation was used to simple gowns with tiny puffed sleeves and delicate flounces around the hem, made of muslin, silk, satin and fine crêpe and over-gowns of gauze — not these stiff, voluminous antiquated items.

'But, aren't they a little old fashioned, Mama?' she said hesitantly, thinking of the fashion drawing she and Emily enjoyed perusing in the monthly magazines that Mrs Dearden, the wife of the local squire passed on to them.

'Don't worry about that!' Mrs Farrington laughed, seeing her daughters' downcast faces. 'I intend only to have the materials restyled and I am sure we can make use of many of the accessories. As for the rest of your needs,' she added brightly, 'we will purchase them!'

'Oh, Mama! It will cost far too much! I really do think we had better write to Lady Hartridge and tell her that I am unable to go!' Patricia wailed, guilty at the thought of so much money being spent on her.

'Nonsense, Patricia! That is just your impetuous nature of speaking before you think things through properly,' Mrs Farrington said calmly. 'I am looking upon this as an investment. And I do have a little money, left to me by my dear mama, which was put by for such an occasion as this. We can buy some lighter silks and muslins with some of that ... and Mrs Dearden has already recommended the services of the Miss Peters and her sister, who are both excellent seamstresses and they are to come here every day until you have sufficient gowns to satisfy the severest of critics.'

The two elderly sisters, who, fortunately, also enjoyed studying the modern magazines of fashion, lived up to their reputation and, when all was complete Patricia was almost speechless with shock at just how many gowns were considered to be indispensable for a Season in London! There were morning and afternoon dresses, walking dresses, a carriage dress and ball dresses — made from sarsnet, crêpe, fine jaconet muslin, French muslin and Berlin silk.

'And now for the accessories!' Harriet declared.

These were purchased on a wonderful day's expedition to Liverpool's finest emporiums — shawls, mantles and hats; shoes, half-boots, reticules, gloves and stockings. Patricia followed the line of porters carrying their purchases to their carriage in a state of dreamlike stupor, a state that was only dispelled when her mama confided that Uncle William, their papa's elder brother, had offered to lend his family coach to convey Patricia and her chaperone, a certain Miss Quiggley, the no-longer-needed governess of a neighbouring family, to London.

Patricia was surprised by this act of generosity as, although Uncle William genially bestowed a guinea apiece upon his nephews and nieces each Christmas or birthday, he had never had any inclination to share his wealth in any greater manner.

'He was horrified when I told him you were going by stage,' her mama said. 'He will also lend the services of Walter, their elderly coachman, and has offered to make all the arrangements at the various inns and establishments along the way. He has so much more experience of such things than your papa, so what else could I say except, 'Thank you very much!' " I know the coach is rather old and shabby but I am sure it will polish up quite well . . . and it does have your uncle's coat of arms emblazoned on its doors! And he pressed a piece of paper into my hands for you. You can imagine my surprise when I saw it was a bill for twenty pounds!'

The next few weeks flew by as the many details in preparing for a lengthy stay in London were dealt with but the day eventually arrived. The lumbersome coach, smartened up considerably with much labour by Uncle William's men, was quickly loaded and after much kissing, hugs and fervently spoken good wishes, Patricia and Miss Quiggley took their seats. Patricia smiled bravely as the door was slammed shut by the groom.

Her brothers and sisters ran along-side whooping and waving as long as they could keep pace with the carriage but, at last they were left behind and Patricia settled back against the padded, velvet upholstery feeling suddenly bereft. The enormity of the undertaking seemed almost too much to bear.

However, once the familiar scenery was left behind and exciting new landmarks presented themselves, Patricia's natural effervescent nature gradually reasserted itself and her exclamations at new sights in the passing countryside encouraged Miss Quiggley to be bold enough to pass on some of her knowledge gained as a governess to her young charge and the time passed more pleasantly.

Both ladies had little experience of travelling and they felt as though they were journeying in unparalleled style and since the inns and posting-houses that Uncle William had chosen for their overnight stops were clean, wholesome and offering adequate accommodation and refreshments, they were well satisfied. By the time their sixth day's travel had commenced, they felt they were well-seasoned travellers and were, indeed, beginning to tire of the constant tedium of the ponderous journey.

Their arrival at an inn at High Wycombe in Buckinghamshire, the penultimate halt in her uncle's schedule, was greeted with great relief from the travellers, especially as the weather, which had been cold but bright during the fist few days, was relentlessly deteriorating.

'I fear those are snow clouds coming down from the north,' Miss Quiggley ventured to predict when she glanced at the sky prior to retiring for the night.

'Anything will be welcome if it relieves the monotony of this tiresome journey!' Patricia declared. 'I vow I never want to travel in a coach ever again in my life!'

Indeed, tiny snowflakes were dancing in the air the following morning and Patricia hurried outside to twirl around in them as soon as they had completed their breakfast.

'Oh, dear, Miss Farrington! Do you

think we should rest here another night until we know which way the weather will go?' Miss Quiggley wondered, when Patricia returned inside with snowflakes glistening in her hair and over her shoulders.

The innkeeper, when approached for his advice, also advised caution. 'You never know, miss, at this time of year. It could turn out quite bad.'

'Nonsense!' Patricia exclaimed. 'Why, it is nothing but a small flurry! Nothing like the winter snow we have at home! No, we have taken long enough on this journey. Let us press on! I have such a longing to arrive in London!'

Their coachman was easily persuaded and, for the first few hours of the day, their optimism seemed justified. However, when they halted at a small hostelry for their luncheon, the snow had thickened and even Patricia felt it prudent to break their journey there for the night. However, when asked, the hostel-keeper shook his head.

'All my rooms is taken,' he regretfully

said. 'But there is another inn not much more than a couple of miles along the road. If your coachman gets a move on, he will have you there in no time at all.'

So he might, if the road had been kept in good repair. Unfortunately, it had not and the fallen snow already covered many of the deep ruts. On a particularly tight left-hand bend that loomed out of the swirls of snow at the last minute, the nearside front wheel dropped down into a deep rut and the carriage tilted to the side.

Walter did his best but the age of the coach and the poor condition of the road, plus the covering of snow, made his efforts futile. The coach lurched sideways, prevented from falling further only by the strength of the under-carriage. Knowing the limits of that particular old piece of timber, Walter leaped down from his driving seat, glad to see that the groom, who had been huddled under his cape on the rear perch, had done likewise.

Both Patricia and Miss Quiggley

screamed when the coach lurched over to the side and they were thrown against the nearside wall of the carriage, where they remained in some disarray, stunned by the shock of the moment to be able to move. However, when Walter pulled open the offside door and said urgently, 'Tha'd best get out, misses!' Patricia immediately hauled herself into a more upright position.

A moment later, Patricia found herself more than calf-deep in powdery snow with a weeping Miss Quiggley soon at her side.

'I knew we should not have progressed onwards!' Miss Quiggley lamented over and over. 'Whatever are we to do, Miss Farrington?'

'We must find some shelter!' Patricia said decisively, glancing about them as if expecting a hostelry to somehow make itself apparent.

'Ah saw some gates not twenty paces back, miss,' the groom volunteered. 'Ah reckon them's our best bet!'

'Oh, dear! Do you think that will be

quite proper?' Miss Quiggley protested nervously, conscious not only of the impropriety of knocking on some private person's door requesting hospitality but also of their now state of dishabillée.

'Of course it is, Miss Quiggley!' Patricia confidently declared. 'Why, no-one would leave so much as a dog outside in this atrocious weather! Come, follow me!'

At which, she picked up the hem of her travelling dress and began to plough her way through the snow in the given direction.

2

At that very moment, within the double-fronted stone residence set some distance back from the road, Lord Jeremy Fulford was turning gloomily away from viewing the falling snow through the front library window. He grimaced ruefully at his host, Mr Gervais Darvill.

'Looks like our evening drive into High Wycombe has been cancelled for us! And the hunt tomorrow! So, what other delights have you lined up for us?' He turned back towards the window and made an exaggerated pretence of looking behind the nearest heavy long curtain. 'I don't suppose there's any chance of there being a couple of opera girls hiding away somewhere?'

Gervais, the more soberly dressed of the two, leaned a raised elbow against the mantelpiece and regarded his friend with some amusement. 'You suppose quite rightly, Jeremy. As you know, I prefer to keep my women and serious hunting quite separate.'

'Indeed you do, Gervais. In fact, the talk is that you are keeping your women extremely separate from everyone at the moment and the on-dit is that you either have someone very special whom you are keeping to yourself or that you are determined to live like a monk for the remainder of your life.'

Gervais frowned and raised a cynical eyebrow. 'And everything the 'gossips' discuss and pass on must be true, I suppose! There must be very little happening in town if they have nothing better to talk about than my 'amours'. I am surprised you give them the time of day, Jeremy.'

'Told 'em it were a bag of moon-shine, Gerv, but you know what the old tabbies are like! And there's often a smidgen of truth in what they say!'

Gervais winced at his friend's short-ened version of his name. He eyed.

Jeremy coolly, his right eyebrow raised. 'What? As much as that, eh?'

Jeremy laughed, emboldened by their long friendship to add, 'Well, people can't help wondering. You haven't been seen with anyone of note for quite some time. Not since the dashing Miss Grantham disappeared off the scene. I bet she dug deep holes in your pocket!'

Gervais's eyebrows rose even higher, a fact which ought to have warned Jeremy that he was in danger of intruding too far into his friend's private affairs, but he was saved from a cutting reply by a discreet knock on the door as the butler apologetically entered the room.

'I beg your pardon for disturbing you, sir, but a carriage has come to grief outside the gates and the two ladies it bore are begging shelter from the inclement weather and maybe some assistance to enable them to continue on their way as soon as conditions improve.'

Gervais's facial expression betrayed

no emotion, although his eyes hardened slightly. However, when he spoke, it was to say calmly, 'Certainly, Rawcliffe. Conduct them to the saloon to the warmth of the fire and ask Mrs Adams to attend to their needs. Oh, and ask Morton to assess the state of the carriage, will you? I am sure he will be able to get it back on the road in no time at all!'

Gervais turned back to his friend as though the matter concerned him no further. Rawcliffe bowed and was about to withdraw from the room but was halted by Jeremy's exclamation of, 'Oh, I say! That's too shabby by far, Gervais! Here we are, bereft of company, and you deny us the pleasure of unexpected visitors! What sort of ladies are they, Rawcliffe? Young? Pretty?'

Rawcliffe was used to his lordship's informality and replied solemnly, 'One is young, milord . . . and, yes, very pretty, I'm sure. The other is of somewhat more years and is, no doubt, her travelling companion.'

'Then show them in here, Rawcliffe! I insist on them being treated with due civility!' Lord Fulford cried, his face brightening.

Rawcliffe glanced at his master for confirmation and, when Gervais nodded his assent with a show of indifference, he bowed out of the room to do as he was bidden.

'Really, Gervais! I swear you are like a dog in a manger today! How can you not be overjoyed at the prospect of our evening being enlivened by such unexpected company?'

'Let's say I am tired of being hunted by a perpetual stream of beauties who have no other aim than to get their hands upon my substantial wealth!' Mr Darvill responded with some weariness in his voice. 'You can have no idea of the tricks they employ to gain my attention . . . tripping over when I am within arm's reach of saving them; fluttering their eyelids and claiming to need a breath of air in the crush of the ballroom — even swooning in my arms in the hope of being carried into an ante-room, where, no doubt, they hope to entrap me into feeling obliged to protect their good name by offering them mine! Which is a false hope, for I have no intention of being bamboozled into making an offer of marriage by anyone! And now, this scheming female has even followed me into the country in this atrocious weather and had a 'mishap' in front of my gates! I'll have none of it, Jeremy!'

Outside the room, Patricia's eyes widened with indignation as this slur upon her character sounded through the slightly open door. She wished the floor would open and swallow her, but the butler had pushed open the door and stood aside to let the two ladies pass in front of him. 'Miss Farrington and Miss Quiggley, gentlemen. Ladies, Mr Gervais Darvill and Lord Fulford!' he murmured before bowing his way out of the room.

The eyes of the two gentlemen were centred on Patricia, who looked extremely fetching in her velvet cloak, with the ruched hood now flung back to reveal her tousled chestnut ringlets framing her rosy cheeks. For a fleeting moment, a light of appreciation shone in both sets of masculine eyes, but the light was swiftly dimmed in the taller of the two as he stepped forward and made a brief bow.

'Your servant, ma'am.'

Patricia could see at a glance that he was dressed as elegantly as any gentleman she had seen. His coat of saxe-blue superfine had been tailored to perfection; an elaborately fastened necktie fell in soft folds; cream pantaloons rippled over the firm muscles of his thighs; and his Hessian boots with a shine that did credit to his valet.

The younger man stepped forward. 'Jeremy Fulford, at your service, ma'am!'

Still embarrassed by the slur on her character, Patricia's cheeks were bright and she cast down her eyes demurely as she bobbed a curtsey to the two men but, trained to be polite to her seniors, she arose from her curtsey and advanced towards the taller man, smiling prettily.

'How do you do?' she began politely. 'I am sorry to intrude upon you in this fashion but our carriage has, unfortunately, broken down right outside your gates and, what with the falling snow and everything, I must beg of you some assistance.'

Her voice petered out as the bland expression on Mr Darvill's face dissolved her confidence. 'I beg your pardon . . . for having presumed upon your hospitality, sir,' she faltered.

'By no means,' Mr Darvill said coolly. 'I have already sent instructions for my men to assess the damage to your carriage. I am sure they will soon have you speeding on your way. It isn't far to the next hostelry.'

'The next hostelry?' Lord Fulford exclaimed, drawing Patricia's eyes towards him. She felt an instinctive smile curving her lips. Here was a man after her brother Thomas's heart; a man of extreme fashion, if the height of the points of his collar and the bold designs of his jacket were to be believed.

'What can you be thinking of, Gervais, with snow falling as thickly as it is?' the man continued. 'It ain't fit for ladies to be out in it!'

'Indeed it isn't,' Gervais Darvill agreed with a cynical twist to his lips. 'That being so, I am sure my housekeeper will be able to sort out a couple of rooms for you, ladies.' He included Miss Quiggley in his polite smile and nodded almost imperceptibly over their heads to Rawcliffe, who needed no repeated instructions to inform him of his next duty. 'And I will send men to bring in your travelling boxes.'

'Thank you, sir,' Patricia said a little stiffly, feeling embarrassed by the man's lack of welcome. Why, her papa had been known to set a tramp at their table, never mind two obviously genteel ladies, however bedraggled! Her indignation against their reluctant host was

mounting. He deserved a touch of his own game!

Accordingly, she tossed back her head and smiled brightly. Those who knew her well would have been warned by the glint of mischief sparkling in her eyes that some indiscretion was afoot.

'La! I can tell by your reaction to our unwarranted intrusion that you suffer a great deal from such invasions of your privacy!' she directed at Mr Darvill. 'How I sympathise! For I suffer in exactly the same way! Most people can have no idea how those of us endowed with great fortune simply long for anonymity.'

'Really?' Mr Darvill raised his lorgnette and coolly regarded her flushed face.

Patricia bristled under his gaze and it occurred to her to wonder if Mr Darvill knew exactly what she was up to. Not one to give in without a fight, she immediately elevated her chin and, although it was difficult to look down her nose at someone who towered a

foot above her height, she managed to convey the attitude she desired.

Mr Darvill stifled the chuckle that rose unbidden in his throat. Most young ladies visibly wilted under such a gaze, whereas Miss Farrington showed herself ready for battle. Maybe he had misjudged her?

A quiet knock at the door prevented any further conversation on the matter and a homely female figure, whom Patricia correctly assumed to be Mr Darvill's housekeeper, stepped into the room.

'Ah, here is Mrs Adams to escort you to your rooms,' Mr Darvill greeted the woman's entrance. 'I trust all will be satisfactory. We will be having a simple dinner in just over an hour's time. You are very welcome to join us.'

Welcoming the distraction, Patricia bobbed a brief curtsey. 'Thank you. That is most kind of you. Come, Miss Quiggley.'

They followed Mrs Adams up the wide staircase and were shown into a

set of two adjoining rooms, separated only by a small bathroom. Fires were already burning in the grates, the curtains drawn against the now darkening sky and a tray of tea and biscuits set on a side table. They were handed into the care of a housemaid, who helped them out of their wet garments, which she then took down to the kitchen to be dried.

As soon as the maid was out of the room, Miss Quiggley, admonished Patricia for her impetuous claim. 'Oh, Miss Farrington! Whatever got into you, saying such things about having a great fortune? What would your mama say?'

'It will be of no account!' Patricia said airily. 'Once they are in town I dare say they will forget all about us! Now, let us refresh ourselves and prepare for dinner. For I declare I am quite famished!'

Patricia chose a simple gown of pale blue muslin and, with their hair tidied, they enjoyed a cup of hot tea and warmed themselves briefly in front of the coals. When they heard a gong sound downstairs they made their way down the stairs to rejoin the gentlemen.

The 'simple' dinner almost took Patricia's breath away, as she knew that the vast array would feed her entire family for a number of days. However, she made every effort not to betray her awe as she sipped the light cream of asparagus soup with croutons, followed by fillets of Dover sole served with an Italian sauce; chicken breasts cooked in a béchamel sauce; a glazed ham and a raised mutton pie. Dishes of lightly cooked vegetables and side dishes containing a selection of garnishes and subtle sauces were placed at each end of the table.

The glass of champagne was almost her undoing. It led her to dismiss her doubts as to the wisdom of her claim to riches and her loosened tongue embellished the fact that she was visiting her Godmother, Lady Hartridge, with the added information that it was in order to escape the attentions and pursuits of her many suitors, drawn to her side, and frequently on their knees at her feet, by the prospect of being the sole inheritor of the fortunes of her many uncles.

She sighed with relish, once again into her imagined role of a targeted heiress. She sighed and spread her hands in a declamatory gesture. 'I declare, having so great a fortune can be a heavy burden to bear at times! You never know whether you are admired for yourself or for the wealth you represent! How I wish at times to be a simple country girl!'

'Oh, you will never be that, Miss Farrington!' Jeremy passionately declared. 'What do you say, Gervais?'

Mr Darvill, who had been listening to this exchange in cynical silence, gravely bowed his assent. 'I am sure you are correct in that assumption, Jeremy.' He turned to address Patricia. 'What a fortunate encounter you have had in coming here, Miss Farrington! Lord Fulford has the ear of all society! A word from him will gain you admittance to the highest of circles. Why, you are made already!'

'Oh!'

This statement alarmed Patricia more than a little. She hadn't thought that far ahead. Still, it was too late to retract her statement now. Her befuddled brain sought to retrieve the situation. 'Oh, I beg of you! I spesh . . . speshifically wish to remain unknown in London. I long for people to get to know me for myself — not for my fortune!'

She hiccupped as the bubbles of the champagne tickled her nose and then giggled when Lord Fulford took hold of her hand and raised it to his lips as he replied gallantly, 'You will be the toast of society, Miss Farrington!'

After the first course dishes were removed, Rawcliffe ushered in the maids carrying a variety of pastries, a cream jelly, tiny almond biscuits and a dish of fruits. Patricia felt compelled by good manners to sample a little of whatever was offered to her but at the end of the meal felt she would not need to eat again for a week!

Just after Miss Quiggley murmured that she felt it was time for them to retire to their rooms, Rawcliffe brought the good news that Mr Darvill's men had righted their carriage and it had been towed around to the rear yard, where the horses were stabled with those belonging to Mr Darvill and Lord Fulford.

'So, all we need now is an improvement in the weather and you will be able to set out on your final leg of your journey to London, Miss Farrington,' Mr Darvill smiled amiably, giving Patricia the impression that the prospect of their departure rested happily upon him. 'You are welcome to stay until the roads are safely passable,' he continued calmly, a slight twinkle in his eyes making Patricia wonder if her ungracious thoughts of him were visible on her face.

'Unfortunately, Lord Fulford and I must return to town tomorrow . . . No, no, have no fear, ma'am,' he addressed to Miss Quiggley, who had gasped in alarm at his statement. 'His lordship and I have had much practice in riding in the snow and, once we are at High Wycombe, the roads will be more passable.'

He ignored the fact that Lord Fulford had also gasped in surprise at his announcement of their departure on the morrow and now included him in his bland gaze that he swept around the table. The intensity of that gaze as it lingered upon him convinced Jeremy that he need not consider contradicting the statement. 'And, since we must be away first thing in the morning, we must say our goodbyes before we retire.'

'Then I must thank you kindly for all your assistance, Mr Darvill,' Patricia said at once, keeping her voice steady with much concentration. 'You have been very ... hic ... gracious in offering us your hospitality.' Her cheeks were highly flushed as she rose from her seat and held out her hand. 'Thank you so much.'

'The pleasure is all mine, Miss Farrington. I am happy to have made your acquaintance and I look forward to calling upon you when you are established with Lady Hartridge.'

As it hadn't occurred to her that he might personally know her Godmother, it wasn't evident whether Patricia's, 'Oh!' of surprise was caused by his words or the fact that he raised her hand to his lips and brushed her fingers with the lightest of touch. Whichever, she tried to hide her agitation by sinking into a curtsey and lowering her eyes . . . though nothing could hide her heightened colour.

Lord Fulford also made his bow, echoing Mr Darvill's promise of visiting her in town. As the ladies departed, the two men stood silently for a moment, the room suddenly seeming empty of all life and light. To ease the moment, Gervais, took out his snuff box and flicked it open, offering it to his friend before taking a pinch of it himself.

'What a delightful creature!' Jeremy exclaimed, still looking towards the doorway as if hoping she might return. 'But, the name . . . Farrington? I cannot recall hearing of the family before, can you? They must be a northern family, perhaps?'

'Really, Jeremy!' Gervais drawled in surprised tones. He delayed inhaling the pinch of snuff he held delicately between his thumb and first finger. 'You have never heard of the Farrington fortune? You amaze me!'

3

More snow had fallen overnight making the world outside Patricia's bedroom window into a winter wonderland of pristine white, broken only by the stark outline of partly obliterated tree trunks and snow-laden branches.

Patricia looked at the scene with a mixture of awe and dismay. The roads had been bad enough the previous afternoon. Now they would be totally impassable. She ran through the small bathroom to Miss Quiggley's room.

'Miss Quiggley! I fear we are destined to be isolated here for a week at least!'

Miss Quiggley threw up her hands. 'Oh, dear! Mr Darvill and Lord Fulford will be snow-bound here with us and Lady Hartridge will wonder what has become of us, Miss Farrington! The impropriety of the situation will spoil your chances of making a suitable match! Whatever will your mama say? Oh dear! I fear I will never get a new position after this!'

Patricia immediately felt contrite. She took the elder lady's hands in her own and crouched at her bedside. 'You are right, Miss Quiggley. I apologise to you . . . and I vow I will never act so impulsively again!'

And, at that moment, she truly meant it.

To their relief, tempered in some measure by slight disappointment on Patricia's part, they learned that the two gentleman had departed the previous evening straight after dinner when they realised that more snow was due to fall. Rawcliffe had no doubt that they would have reached the next hostelry at least and would arrive in town within a couple of days.

'Mr Darvill begs you to excuse his absence but cordially extends the hospitality of his abode to you ladies,' Rawcliffe concluded.

It was indeed a week before they

were able to complete their journey to London. A week of such boredom that Patricia never wished to repeat. The household staff gave them every attention and treated them as invited guests, but it was a bachelor establishment with very few occupations suitable for ladies of whatever age.

Walter and the groom were well-cared for with the outdoor staff but they, too, were relieved when the thaw set in and it became evident that they would be able to depart on the morrow.

After the near silence of the snow-bound week, neither of the two ladies was prepared for the noisy bustle of the London streets — the rumble of the coach wheels on the cobbled streets, only slightly muted by the thawing mush at the edges of the street; the shouts of coachmen and other travellers; the barking of dogs; the calls of children and street vendors — all intermingling to create a clamour of sound.

The streets widened as they progressed towards the more genteel parts in the West End of London. Patricia knew that her Godmother lived in Duke Street and, as the coach was drawn to a standstill, was impressed to see that the house, built entirely of unrendered stone, unlike some of its neighbours, was at least four storeys high. She craned back her neck to admire front façade, decorated as it was by elegant, tall, carved pillars. It looked very grand.

'Don't gape, dear,' Miss Quiggley whispered as she joined her charge on the paving stones. 'Come, let us proceed up the steps. The servants will attend to our baggage.'

Lady Hartridge's butler, whom Patricia later learned was called Kettering, was already standing majestically at the open door having been summoned hence by one of the footmen. As Patricia picked up the skirt of her travelling robe and began to ascend the steps, a junior footman was already hurrying down the steps in order to direct Walter how to take the coach round to the rear courtyard.

'Welcome to Lady Hartridge's residence, Miss Farrington,' Kettering greeted her. 'Lady Hartridge awaits you in the drawing room. If you will come this way.'

He led the way up a grand curved staircase to the first floor. Large, elaborately framed oil paintings of various scenes decorated the walls and, at the top of the stairs the landing divided into two. Patricia swung her glance around, overwhelmed by the imposing elegance. Kettering approached a double door, both halves of which he opened and resonantly announced their names.

Patricia stepped into the light, spacious room a little nervously but hadn't time to take in much of its style and décor as a rather plump lady, much smaller than herself, hurried forwards, her face beaming with delight. Schooled by her mama how to greet a lady of rank, Patricia sank into a low curtsey.

Lady Hartridge instantly raised her up and enveloped her to her ample bosom. 'Oh, my dear Miss Farrington! I am so relieved to see you here at last! What a journey you must have had!' She threw up her hands, exclaiming. 'What a to-do! Your mama must be out of her mind with worry, but now I can write to let her know you have arrived safely. You must be perished! We expected you might arrive today. Mr Darvill said it would probably be five or six days before the roads were clear enough for a heavy coach . . . and he was quite right!'

The mention of Mr Darvill's name threw Patricia into confusion. 'M . . . Mr Darvill c . . . called here?' she stammered.

'Yes, indeed. I'm sure it was very civil of him for he was under no obligation to do so.' Lady Hartridge tapped Patricia lightly on her wrist. 'Did he appear to like you?' she asked roguishly. 'I am sure he did, such a pretty thing that you are.'

Patricia remembered Mr Darvill's coolness and the words she had overheard ... his suspicions of her motives in visiting his house ... and she wondered if she should admit her impulsive pretence of being an heiress. Oh dear! If only she could turn back the clock! But the moment passed with her confession unuttered.

'I ... I do not think he was very impressed with me,' she faltered, 'and I thought him very proud and haughty. Lord Fulford was very agreeable with me, though.'

'Oh, you needn't be setting your cap at Lord Fulford, my dear. He may have a title but he is a bit short in the pocket. He needs to marry into money!'

Patricia felt her cheeks flushing. 'Indeed, ma'am, I don't think of setting my cap at either Lord Fulford or Mr Darvill. I am sure it would not be well received. Why, they left the house as soon as dinner was over, even though they must have had to plough their way through the snowdrifts!'

'Nonsense! They were being careful of your reputation, so do not mention to anyone that you stayed overnight, indeed for a week, in Mr Darvill's hunting lodge. It could give people the wrong idea entirely and make you an outcast before you begin. But what a start it has given you over all the other young ladies of this Season! Mamas have been pushing their daughters into his path for any number of Seasons but none has managed to leg-shackle him yet! However, we must be realistic. Mr Darvill is out of your reach as far as the marriage mart goes. Money marries money, you know!'

Patricia listened in dismay, realising that she had more than likely ruined her chances of attracting anyone to think favourably of her. Oh, dear! How disappointed her mama would be . . . and what a waste of the money she had laid out upon her.

Seeing her woeful expression, Lady Hartridge determined to restore the spirits of her young protégée. 'But, no more of that. I will ring for one of the maids to show you to your rooms and, later, we will talk about all that we are going to do whilst you are here in London with me . . . and, tomorrow, I shall take you shopping! Oh, we are going to have such fun together!'

The following day, Lady Hartridge waited only until after Miss Quiggley's departure to the home of a distant cousin with whom she was to stay whilst seeking new employment, before she commanded Patricia to attire herself suitably for the cold weather as they were going to the shops immediately.

Patricia's rare trips to the emporiums of Liverpool and Southport were completely diminished by the grandeur of the London shops. The range of goods was far superior and the prices took her breath away but she limited herself to buying a new pair of gloves and some ribbons to decorate her bonnet. However, she enjoyed the outing and later wrote a letter home to her family describing all the colours and textures of the fabrics she had seen and the wonderful displays in the shop windows.

Lady Hartridge was keen to discuss her plans for Patricia's introduction to Society. 'Now, my dear, although I intend to try to obtain vouchers from Almack's for you, I have decided to hold a small gathering here at my home in order to introduce you to some of my friends and acquaintances. Just a small gathering, maybe twenty or thirty guests, including, of course, some young ladies who may like you to be their friend and some young gentlemen though we mustn't be too ambitious, of course, bearing in mind your lack of a marriage portion.'

'However, one can't have too many acquaintances! There is nothing more awkward than attending a Ball and not knowing anyone else who is there!'

Patricia agreed there was not but when Lady Hartridge placed Mr Darvill's name at the top of her list, she found herself protesting against the inclusion of that particular gentleman.

'For I am sure he is not at all likely to come to my party, I would much prefer you did not to invite him, ma'am.'

'Not invite him? When his very presence would make it an instant success?' Lady Hartridge said in incredulous tones. Her voice softened when she noted Patricia's earnest expression. 'Ah, I see you are too modest a young lady and you fear to imply that you think too much of your short acquaintance with him! Have no worry on that score! Why, if he doesn't choose to come, he will just toss the invitation aside and think no more of it! I'm sure I do so all the time!'

Patricia was relieved to have the matter dropped.

Two days later, Lord Fulford paid a morning call, much to Lady Hartridge's delight. 'For although he and his family may be at low water, he has friends in the right places.'

He strode into the drawing room with the confidence bred into him.

'Miss Farrington! Delighted to meet up with you again. You are looking wonderfully well! Thought we might go for a turn around the park one afternoon now the weather is improving . . . with your leave, of course, Lady Hartridge.'

Lady Hartridge bowed her consent and Lord Fulford rattled on about his prime bits of blood and how he meant to cut a fine dash with his new team. He reminded Patricia so much of Thomas that she found him easy to talk to and accepted the many compliments he paid her with little conviction that they were any more than social niceties, complimenting him in return on the complicated folds of his neck-tie, knowing well how many hours he must have spent in front of a mirror perfecting the intricacies of its creation.

At the end of the accepted half-hour, Lord Fulford took his leave full of good spirit and determination to speak admirably to all of his acquaintances of the latest new face in town.

He was the first of number of visitors and Lady Hartridge was gratified to think that her groundwork of dropping hints to her friends of her Goddaughter's impending visit had fallen on such fertile ground. It was the same when they took a carriage drive in Hyde Park. They were hailed and acknowledged by many of the 'Ton', pleasantries were exchanged and promises of visits avowed.

'How kind everyone is!' Patricia declared to her Godmother. 'I had feared that London Society would pay scant attention to a northern newcomer. Why, more people stop their carriages to talk to us than in my hometown!'

'It pays to have connections, my dear,' Lady Hartridge said a little smugly. 'I am more than happy to lend you my patronage and . . . Oh, now smile prettily, my dear. Here comes Mr Darvill himself!'

Patricia's breath caught in her throat. She had known this meeting must happen at some point since Mr Darvill had paid his initial call to inform her Godmother of her delayed arrival, but she hadn't thought it would be in so public a place.

'Good afternoon, Miss Farrington. What a fine day it is! I trust you and your travelling companion were comfortable during your unexpected stay in High Wycombe?'

Patricia hoped he wasn't about to shame her by making some side reference to her outrageous claim to be an heiress and, in consequence, was afraid that a tell-tale blush of embarrassment might steal across her cheeks. Remarkably though, she remained cool and, instead of breaking their glance as she was longing to do, she tilted her chin a little higher and held his gaze.

'Very much so, sir. I am indebted to you for your kindness. Thank you.'

His eyes were as dark as melted treacle and Patricia felt she could detect a glint of humour in their depth. Could he sense her thoughts?

So she dismissed her fear and held

his gaze. A glint of something, she wasn't sure what, seemed to shine in the dark depths of his eyes, though it was gone when, with an inclination of his head, he gallantly replied, 'I was happy to be of service, Miss Farrington. No-one could have foreseen such inclement weather.'

Maybe her portrayal of an imminent heiress had been convincing? And, after all, what harm had it done? Her escapade had brought her to his attention and it was very gratifying to see the curious looks they were receiving — envious looks, some of them, Patricia couldn't help noticing.

Mr Darvill's stallion was impatiently pawing the ground and Patricia was both relieved and sorry when Mr Darvill gathered the reins in one hand and tipped his hat again with the other as he bade them, 'Good day.'

Lady Hartridge leaned back against the seat beaming with delight. 'That was very opportune!' she murmured. 'Did you notice the regard that was given to us when Mr Darvill was addressing us? I do believe you will find many doors open to you after this! Well done, my dear!'

She was even more gratified on their return to Duke Street when it was discovered that Mr Darvill had made a house call prior to meeting them in the park and had left his card.

'And you know what that means!' she declared with great satisfaction.

Patricia was puzzled.

'N . . . no,' she admitted. 'Is it important?'

'Important! It is the very best! It means we are now able to invite Mr Darvill to your party after all! Oh, what a triumph it will be if he comes!'

4

Patricia had no great hopes that Mr Darvill would come to her party. Why should he, even if he believed her pretence of being an heiress she was of no great account and, in spite of the fact that he had paved the way for others to acknowledge her by his gallant action in the park, he had made no further call. Consequently, although Lady Hartridge made much about sending his invitation by hand delivery, Patricia refused to get drawn into her Godmother's anticipation of his attendance.

Her days were full of excitement and Lady Hartridge's drawing room was seldom bereft of visitors. Mamas brought their daughters to befriend Miss Farrington; young men called to make her acquaintance, many demanding introduction from Jeremy Fulford, who, after bringing one or two friends, began to visit on his own; other visitors left their cards if they called while Lady Hartridge and Patricia were on one of their many excursions to the London stores or driving in the parks.

On each return to the house more invitations to the party were dispatched and its venue was changed from the salon to the ballroom and more lavish plans introduced. Patricia's pleas for prudence were brushed aside.

'Nonsense, dear. It will be the 'talk' of the Season!' Lady Hartridge exclaimed, her face wreathed in smiles. 'Oh, how I used to long for a daughter to launch into society! It isn't the same with a son, you know. They make their own way and rarely listen to their mamas. Even my dear Nicholas is more interested in travelling on the continent with his friends than spending time here in London looking for a wife! I have my eye on Lord Ellington's eldest daughter for him, you know, but she will have been snapped by some other young man if he doesn't make his suit known!'

'Is she a great beauty, ma'am?'

'Not noticeably so — but the family have both title and money. As for beauty, that is an added bonus when put with the other two, and it's not often all three are seen together!' She sighed deeply but then dismissed her wistful expression and brightly tapped Patricia's arm. 'At least no-one can fault you in that department, my dear! Now, what do you think of my idea of swathes of pink silk looped along the sides of the supper tables? Now, when can I find time to take it to the Misses Grainger's shop in Bond Street and select which flowers to use?'

'Maybe I could go?' Patricia volunteered eagerly, longing to be able to go somewhere on her own. Much as she appreciated all that Lady Hartridge was doing for her, her constant talk about people's wealth or lack of it and her comparisons of every personage mentioned became a little wearisome at times.

Lady Hartridge gave the suggestion some consideration and finally nodded her agreement. 'Yes, that's an ideal suggestion. I think your taste in the matter of colour is the same as mine. You will take Kitty, of course, and the town coach. Pilling will drive you. Do remember that London is greatly different from Southport and undesirables are always on the lookout for a green-stick.'

Patricia rushed upstairs and informed Kitty of their impending visit. Kitty was as excited as she was and she swiftly sorted out a suitable dress for Patricia to wear.

There was no restraint between mistress and maid and both exclaimed in delight at the quite ordinary sights and sounds of the busy London streets. The wheels rumbled over the cobbles and the voices of the vendors who were calling out their wares became discernible as the crowded streets in the inner city made their pace slower. 'Hot muffins — four a penny! Oranges! Sweet oranges! Baked potatoes!'

Patricia bobbed her head out of the open window so that she might see the sights and hear the sounds more readily but drew back immediately when a small arm was thrust towards her face and a child's voice pleaded, 'A penny, miss! Just a penny!'

'Oh, the poor child!' she exclaimed.

'Take no notice, miss. There're beggars everywhere. They'd rob you as soon as you've stopped to help them.'

'Oh, surely not! The poor child must be hungry!'

'He probably is, miss, but you can't help them all.'

'Maybe not, but it touches my heart to see them thus.'

The carriage eventually drew to a halt and Kitty leaped down and turned to lower the step for Patricia to descend in a more ladylike manner. Patricia looked for the familiar frontage of the haberdashery shop that she had visited only a few days previously with her

Godmother but she realised it had been impossible for Pilling to halt outside the Misses Grainger's premises.

'It's just back there, miss,' Pilling informed her, pointing with his folded whip.

Patricia thanked him and glanced around with interest at the tall buildings, since, on her previous visits with Lady Hartridge, they had swept inside the stores without delay. The sun was shining and Patricia was in no hurry to return to Duke Street.

The two girls paused at every window and pressed their noses against the glass, exclaiming excitedly at the variety of goods for sale. At last, they arrived at the haberdashery shop and entered its dim interior. It reminded Patricia of the story of Aladdin's Cave with its multitude of shelves, cupboards and drawers.

Patricia explained her errand and one of the elderly spinster sisters guided Patricia to a chair whilst the other enlisted the help of their assistant to carry bales of pink silk to the nearby counter so that Patricia could make her selection. Samples of silk flowers were then brought for her perusal and a mixture of pink ones and cream ones were tentatively held together in posy-form with a few stalks of green silk leaves until they reached an agreed arrangement.

Once more out in the sunshine, she glanced up and down the street.

'It's far too lovely to go straight home!' she declared. 'Isn't that shop where Lady Hartridge ordered the sweetmeats and fruit ices for my party somewhere near here? What was it called? Hunter's . . . or something like that?'

'Gunter's, miss . . . and, yes, it's just along there in Berkley Square.'

'Good! Let's have a treat, shall we? I have hardly spent any of the money my Uncle William gave to me.' She patted the reticule that hung on her arm. 'A fruit ice will be very welcome on this beautiful day. Run and tell Pilling where we are going, Kitty. I am sure he will be able to turn the carriage around somewhere and he can meet us there.'

As Kitty ran over to where Pilling was keeping the restless horses in check, Patricia began to saunter slowly westward along Bond Street. The sound of horses hooves and carriage wheels rattling over the cobbled road almost drowned out the other sounds of the city and Patricia was hardly aware of the clatter of running feet behind her until a push in her back sent her staggering against the window of the store she was passing. She felt a tug at her reticule and she clutched it fiercely with her other hand, at the same time twisting around to face her attacker.

He was a youth of about fourteen years, his thin face grimy and his hair matted to his head. His threadbare clothes hung on his thin body and, if the circumstances had not been so alarming, Patricia would have felt sorry for him and probably would have opened her reticule to give him some money. As it was, however, his fierce expression made her want to back away . . . which she did, still holding tightly to her reticule, inadvertently pulling the youth towards her.

He, in turn, braced his body away from her and gave a strong tug at the reticule with both his hands. Patricia could feel her grip on it loosening. Its straps were still looped over her left arm and, as it slipped from her grasp, she instinctively struck out with her right fist in the manner that she had seen Thomas and her cousin, Harry, employ when having 'friendly' fights between themselves. They had never allowed her to join in this particular game but that hadn't stopped her practising their moves in the privacy of her room.

To her great satisfaction, her clenched fist struck the youth's nose and he staggered backwards, his grip on her reticule broken. The expression on his face was almost comical. It was a mixture of surprise, pain and reluctant admiration.

His hands clutched at his nose and

Patricia could see blood spurting through his fingers. Her own hand hurt, too, and she rubbed her knuckles with her other hand as she took a step forward . . . with the foolish intention of apologising to the lad as she realised, too late, that she acted against her father's teaching of 'turning the other cheek'!

The lad mistook her intention as one of further aggression and he continued to back away, holding out one hand in front of him to ward off her next attack. When the attack didn't come, he spun around, intending to make his getaway along the crowded flag way — but, instead, ran right into the firm body of a gentleman. Before he realised what was happening, the man had grasped the collar of his thin jacket and had lifted him off his feet by the scruff of his neck. As he dangled helplessly from the man's hand, he heard him say, 'Has the lad harmed you in any way, Miss Farrington?'

Patricia was as much surprised to see

her attacker dangling from the man's hand, as he was to be there.

'Mr Darvill!' she exclaimed, her cheeks burning as she realised that he had witnessed her unladylike behaviour. His expression seemed thunderous. 'I am not usually so aggressive, sir. I . . . I hardly knew what I was doing!'

'Are you hurt?' he repeated, his facial features relaxing slightly at the unexpected nature of her reply.

'N . . . no. Just my knuckles, I think — and that was self-inflicted!'

'Indeed it was!' he replied, smiling openly now.

He realised that a small crowd of passers-by had gathered around them. The attempted robbery had happened very swiftly and it was only now that it was almost over that passers-by were aware that anything untoward had occurred. With a disarming smile and gesture of his hand, Gervais waved them away.

Gervais sensed that shock was about to overcome Miss Farrington. Her face had gone white but she still held herself erect. She needed something to distract her. 'That was a good bit of home-brewed you dealt this rascal!' he drawled. 'Who taught you to fight like that?'

'I watched Thomas and Harry . . . that is . . . '

'Your brothers?' he queried, raising an eyebrow.

'Yes. I mean no. Thomas is my . . . I mean, a brother of one of my friends,' she hastily corrected herself, remembering her false claim. 'Harry is his . . . friend. I . . . er . . . Oh, please excuse me, sir! I hardly know what I am saying.'

Gervais instantly rebuked himself. What a boor he was, quizzing her like this after such an experience! Most young ladies would have been in a faint on the ground in such circumstances! He inclined his head in acceptance of her words.

'Of course,' he agreed. 'It is a good thing to have friends with brothers when one has none of one's own. I apologise. You were very brave.'

Patricia bristled at what seemed to be a patronising acclamation. 'No more than my . . . friends' brothers would have been!'

He bowed. 'You are correct. I apologise again.' He could see the colour returning to her face and knew her crisis was over. 'What shall we do with this little thief, eh?'

'I ain't no thief, mister!'

'Silence lad!'

'I . . . I think you should lower his feet to the ground,' Patricia faltered quietly. 'You are almost choking him, sir.'

'So I am! Is this better, lad?'

He allowed the lad's feet to touch the ground and changed his hold on him to an arm lock.

The boy winced and distress flashed in Miss Farrington's eyes.

'You are still hurting him!' she protested.

Good heavens! What next? 'He tried to rob you!'

'Didn't mean no 'arm to 'er, mister,' the boy whined, making a feeble attempt to wriggle out of his grasp.

'No harm? You attacked her, lad! I saw you!' Good Lord, why was he even arguing his point?

'Probably because he is hungry! Just look at him! He's starving!' Miss Farrington's hands were now on her hips.

People were beginning to stare. How he hated scenes! Some perversity made him continue. 'Letting him go won't stop him starving. He'll only try to rob someone else!'

'I won't, mister! Honest, I won't!' the boy pleaded.

Miss Farrington's mouth opened and closed a few times. Gervais grinned in triumph. Hah! That's got her!

Miss Farrington's eyes narrowed as she weighted his words.

'You are quite right!' she agreed. 'I must take him home with me!' She raised herself on her tiptoes attempting to look above the crowds. 'Now, where is Pilling?'

The lad struggled again to free himself as Miss Farrington made as if to hurry away towards Berkley Square. 'Don't send me with 'er, mister! She drew me cork! I won't be safe with a hell-cat like that!'

'Pilling?' Gervais echoed, still holding on to the lad's collar. His mind was dealing with her decision to take the lad home and he wondered how Lady Hartridge would react to Miss Farrington arriving home with a street urchin in tow.

'My coachman. I sent my maid to tell him that we are going to Gunter's for some fruit ices. Now, I must find him and tell him of our change of plan.'

Gervais had never met such an impetuous young lady. He almost laughed at the absurdity of it all. 'Don't rush away, Miss Farrington, before you have considered whether or not Lady Hartridge will welcome this urchin!' he drawled.

That stopped her. He saw various emotions flicker over her face, ending with defeat. Her whole demeanour sagged.

'No, I forgot. Oh, dear! What are we to do with him? Oh, I know!' Her face brightened. 'You can take him!'

'I? Oh, no, Miss Farrington!'

'Yes, you must. It is exactly what my father would do!'

That took him aback. 'He would?'

'Certainly! We often have tramps and beggars at our table. Oh, dear. I mean, we would if they came knocking on our door, that is.'

Gervais narrowed his eyes. Just what sort of home did the delightful Miss Farrington come from?

'I am not your father!' he growled.

'Well, no . . . but you are very like him in some ways. And he is very kind.' She smiled winningly at him. 'It is the ideal solution! I am sure you could find some sort of position for him.'

Now it was Gervais's turn to open and close his mouth with no words coming forth.

'I can clean boots, mister!' the lad volunteered.

Gervais shuddered. No-one except Hill ever touched his boots!

'Miss! Miss! Is everything all right, miss?' It was Kitty, pushing her way through the pedestrians on the flag way. She arrived looking flustered. 'Sorry I took so long, miss. There seemed a bit of a 'do' and I couldn't get through. Anyway, Pilling said as he knows another way round and he'll meet us at Gunter's.' She suddenly noticed the well-dressed man holding an urchin in an arm-lock. 'What's to do, miss?'

'Nothing is amiss, Kitty. Mr Darvill and I were renewing our acquaintance and he is about to take his leave with his new employee . . . aren't you, Mr Darvill?'

She smiled at him sweetly, the little minx! He tried to glare at her but she didn't wilt under the intensity of his gaze. Indeed, her head tilted a little higher and she increased her smile. Heiress or not, she probably had imperious royal blood coursing through her veins!

He bowed his head briefly in assent. 'As soon as I have decided how to see you safely to your carriage, Miss Farrington . . . since I cannot trust my 'new employee' to stick around if I release him.' Though why he should be concerned if the lad stuck around or not, he didn't know!

'I am quite capable of walking to Gunter's in safety with my maid at my side, Mr Darvill!' Patricia said indignantly.

'I was thinking more of the safety of London's street urchins, Miss Farrington,' Gervais assured her, trying to maintain a straight face. 'By this time next week you might have them all swept up into enforced labour!'

'Oh, no, Mr Darvill! That isn't . . . Oh, you're teasing me, aren't you?'

'I am indeed! But you do see my problem, don't you? As a gentleman, I cannot just abandon you. I am sure your father wouldn't do so!' he added slyly.

She saw the truth of his gibe. 'No, he wouldn't,' she admitted ruefully.

The dilemma was solved for them by the sound of a male voice calling, 'Good afternoon, Miss Farrington! Oh . . . and Mr Darvill, sir!' The latter part was spoken not quite so brightly as Miss Farrington's companion was recognised.

Both Patricia and Mr Darvill looked towards the sound of the voice and saw a landau drawing to a halt alongside them. Seated on the driving seat were two young men about the age of her brother, Thomas, Patricia thought. Their faces were vaguely familiar. Realising that they must have visited her in Lady Hartridge's house, she returned their smile.

'Good afternoon, gentlemen!' she replied. 'I am sorry, I can't quite remember . . .'

'Algernon Albright and Stephen Beresford,' the one nearest to her quickly replied, tipping his hat, whilst the one holding the reins nodded his head towards them. 'Paid a visit to you at Lady Hartridge's on Tuesday, Miss Farrington. Delightful time!' Algernon Albright added, red-faced.

The pair were clearly embarrassed and regretting their impulsive greeting. 'Sorry to intrude,' his glance sweeping across to Mr Darvill. 'Didn't realise. Had your back to us, you know.'

Gervais waved his free hand. 'Never mind all that! I gather you know these two gentlemen, Miss Farrington . . . however slightly?'

'Oh, yes,' Patricia brightly agreed, for she, too, had seen the providence of their arrival. 'Yes, I recognised them instantly.' She beamed at the two young men.

'Then, may I ask you, gentleman, if you would be so kind as to convey Miss Farrington and her maid to Gunter's, where their carriage awaits them. I have . . . er . . . other 'business' to attend to.'

'Certainly, sir!' Algernon eagerly agreed.

Patricia took a step towards him but then turned back to Mr Darvill. She held out her hand, which he took within his. 'Thank you for your kindness, sir. I'm sure you will not regret it. And you, boy . . . ' She fixed him with her eye but was smiling gently. ' . . . work hard for Mr Darvill. For he will let me know how you get on, you know!'

With another smile at the reluctant benefactor, she took her leave, accepting Algernon's hand into the landau and seated herself demurely on the front-facing seat. Kitty seated herself opposite to her and Algernon, under Mr Darvill's stern eye, resisted the temptation to seat himself next to the delightful Miss Farrington and instead resumed his place on the driving seat next to his friend.

5

Gervais glanced down at the scruffy urchin at his side, only now realising that he had released his hold of him at some point in the past few minutes, but the lad had not made his escape.

'Well, lad! You heard all that Miss Farrington had to say and her pleas on your behalf. However, you are not bound over to do as she says and I have no intention of dragging you through the streets of London to where I live. Nor will I be locking you in, if or when we get there. Do you understand? If you wish to be taken into my employment, you will come willingly and will work hard. I will put you in the care of one of my men and if he has any complaint to make about you, you will be dismissed. Do you understand what I am saying?'

The boy nodded, his large eyes round

with awe at his good fortune. 'Yessir! I'll do me best, sir!'

Gervais frowned, wondering just what sort of existence this lad and others like him had. He had never really thought about it. Never had to! But now it had been thrust upon him by Miss Farrington's machinations. That young lady had a lot to answer for!

He realised the lad was watching him anxiously, so he dismissed his thoughts in order to deal with the business in hand. 'Right! I am going to turn around and you will follow me at a distance. If you are not behind me when I reach my destination, I will trust that you have changed your mind and no longer wish to be hired by me.'

With that, Gervais turned and sauntered back along Bond Street, wondering if his 'shadow' would be with him when he arrived at his town house in Park Lane. He nodded to acquaintances, glanced in shop windows, conversed with some friends, tipped his hat to some ladies who bowed their heads towards him from their carriage and, to all and sundry, showed a carefree demeanour.

He was approaching his front steps when he stopped and looked around. Had the lad gone? That would be a relief . . . except Miss Farrington would probably think he was to blame for his departure! No, there he was, leaning against the railings about twenty yards back, scuffing his bare toes in the dust. Well, one thing for sure, he couldn't come in through the front entrance. Wallis would have an apoplectic fit!

He made an ungentlemanlike whistle, a thing he hadn't done for years, and the lad's head jerked up. Gervais beckoned him and the lad came running.

'I'm still 'ere, mister!'

'So I see. Stay where you are and I will send someone to take you around to the back entrance. You need a good scrub before you are allowed into my kitchen.'

'Yer what? Yer said nowt about havin'

to be scrubbed!'

'I'm saying it now! A good scrub and then a bowl of Mrs Cooper's best broth!' He raised a questioning eyebrow. 'It's your decision, of course.'

The lad scowled. 'I s'pose I'll survive it.'

'You will., By the by, what's your name, lad?'

The boy grinned. 'Jimmy! Me mates call me Lucky Jim.'

Gervais's household was taken by storm. Who would have supposed that one small urchin could cause so much disruption? He let out a howl when he realised the tub of hot water was for him to be submerged in and would have made a dash for it had his clothes not already been removed for burning.

He yelled as if in dire pain whilst he was being scrubbed by a non-too-gentle groom, who thought it greatly beneath his dignity to be assigned the task of 'nursemaid' to a filthy street brat, but who knew better than to abuse his position because he knew word of it would get back to his master.

The odd assortment of clean clothes felt strange upon Jimmy's red and tingling body and the boots almost crippled him as he was hustled across the yard and into the warmth of the kitchen, where he forgot his fleeting glimpse of the gate to freedom to his world when the appetising aroma of chicken broth assailed his nostrils and he decided he may as well be fed before he made his get-away.

He was directed to a bench at a well-scrubbed kitchen table, where a bowl of appetising broth awaited him. This he swooped into his hands and gulped its contents down without pause. Then he wiped the back of his hand across his mouth and said, 'By gum! That were good! Is there any more?' And Mrs Cooper refrained from rebuking him for his lack of table manners and decided to mother him instead.

He was then re-assigned into the care of the groom, who took him back to the stables where he was given the task of helping the stable boys to brush out the stalls, clean the tackle and generally be at the beck and call of all his superiors . . . who, at the moment, was everyone, it seemed. The other lads eyed him with suspicion, but Jimmy was no weakling, even though he had been almost floored by a chit of a girl! He stared back belligerently. They might look down on him now but he'd show 'em! He was going up in the world!

Patricia knew none of this. The day of her party, now magnified to the status of *Ball*, was drawing nearer . . . and finally arrived. She tormented herself with thoughts of 'what if no-one came?' 'What if society decided that she wasn't of high enough pedigree' and all the salutations she received daily in the park and visits in Lady Hartridge's drawing-room were simply 'polite' things to do . . . a mere sham to cover their true feelings? How disappointed Lady Hartridge would be! The event must have cost a small fortune! More than her mama and papa spent in a whole year!

'Nonsense, my dear!' Lady Hartridge assured her. 'Why I have received almost a hundred acceptances and if only half of them actually come, the event would be counted a great success!'

By seven o'clock, the ballroom was ready, its glittering decorations twinkling in the candlelight. Chairs and small tables were artistically arranged around the edge of the dance floor; a small orchestra had been hired to play the music; a fabulous supper was laid out in the dining-room; and Kettering was attired in his best uniform to perform the duty of *major domo* as the guests arrived.

Patricia held her nerves in check as Lady Hartridge's own personal maid dressed her hair in a fall of ringlets caught up by a circlet of primroses that matched exactly the colour of her crêpe gown that opened over a slip of white satin. Around her slender neck she wore the single strand of her grandmother's pearls that her mama had thoughtfully lent to her.

A posy of primroses arrived from Lord Fulford and she wondered how he had known which colour she was going to wear — until Kitty's coy smile informed her of his source of knowledge.

Patricia was glad she had carried it down with her when she saw Lord Fulford's delighted smile when he saw it in her hand and he immediately wrote his name twice on her dance card. The ballroom was filling nicely and by ten o'clock there was such a crush that late-comers were obliged to squeeze their way through. In between dances, Patricia was surrounded by eager young beaux and a fair number of young ladies who were happy to be able to show off their charms in the lively circle.

It was supper time when Gervais Darvill made his appearance. His eyes drifted over the colourful throng and his lip curled a little scornfully as he thought of how he had engineered the whole affair with one little sentence! He knew that Jeremy had only mentioned Miss Farrington's 'high expectations' to one or two acquaintances, but Society tittle-tattle had its own way of spreading and now, it seemed, practically the whole of the *ton* was privy to the *secret* of Miss Farrington's fortune. What a fickle and unreliable *force* it was!

Gervais allowed himself a smile of satisfaction. The rumour had ensured a good turnout at Miss Farrington's party and Lady Hartridge, her hand fluttering from her neck to her bosom and back again when he paid her his respects to her, appeared happy to believe that she was amongst the influential inner core of Society.

He wondered if Miss Farrington appreciated his efforts on her behalf. By rights, he should have denounced her as an impostor . . . except, as far as he could ascertain by carefully listening to the gossip, Miss Farrington hadn't said anything to anybody, apart from him and Lord Fulford, to encourage their belief in her fortune. She had appeared to remain the same unspoiled girl with an air of charming naïvety that was endearing her to everybody, even those hard-to-please mamas with daughters of their own to push forward into the limelight.

Had being the centre of all this attention and flattery now gone to Miss Farrington's head? Was she now above herself with airs and graces? Hah! If so, serve her right when her true state of affairs became known and her *courtiers* drifted away. That would teach her to try to bamboozle him!

A pang of guilt assailed his conscience at that unworthy thought. Try though he might to despise Miss Farrington for her impetuous attempt to deceive him, he knew she had been motivated by pique rather than by the desire to pretend to be an heiress. And how many women did he know who would use their feminine charms to beguile him into taking a street urchin into his employ? He could think of none.

He was conscious of whispers about his presence as he threaded his way across the room to where Miss Farrington and several other young ladies were seated surrounded by a dozen or so young men vying with each other to entice her to accept tasty sweetmeats and pastries from their plates.

'Why, gentlemen! I should barely be able to move if I eat all that you offer me!' he heard her lightly declare. 'Here, Sophie, you have this one! And, Dorothea, do accept that piece of chicken from . . . what was your name, sir? Mr Thornton. And yes, Lord Fulford, a glass of lemonade would be very welcome.'

Gervais paused at the edge of the group watching her facial expressions as she divided her attention between those around her and found himself to be quite entranced. It was a few moments before Miss Farrington became aware of his presence and he regretted that he could no longer watch her unseen.

If he had been expecting her to coyly cast down her eyes or to blush with pride at being the recipient of his attention, he would have been disappointed. Her initial reaction of surprise was closely followed by a welcoming smile.

'Mr Darvill! How lovely to see you! I wasn't sure that this would be your sort of pastime. Will you take some refreshment? I am sure someone . . . '

Patricia let her sentence drift off into the air as the young men, most of them overawed by his more mature status, stepped back a pace to allow him room to make his bow, which he did with solemn grace. The simplicity of his perfectly tailored coat and breeches made the other men appear to be dandies with their exaggerated fashions.

A diamond pin embellished the froth of lace at his throat and the fall of lace at his wrists wafted an intriguing scent as he raised her hand to his lips. Her heart was beating so rapidly it was making her feel quite dizzy.

'I am delighted to be here, Miss Farrington,' he said with a dazzling smile. 'Ah! The glass of lemonade! Thank you, Jeremy! And one for Miss Farrington!'

'Oh, I say, Gervais! That's a sham do!' Lord Fulford protested as he relinquished the two glasses.

Mr Darvill ignored the protest and Patricia reached out her hand to accept the proffered glass, hoping no-one would notice how much it was shaking. This man could destroy her character with one sentence.

As if the younger company realised that Mr Darvill made them seem boyish by comparison, they withdrew slightly leaving Patricia alone with her distinguished guest.

'I am pleased to see so many at your Ball,' he smiled. 'You must be very happy to have made so many friends so quickly.'

'Oh, indeed, sir!' she replied demurely. 'Though I am sure it has more to do with Lady Hartridge's friends and acquaintances than with anything I might have done. She is being very kind to me.'

Gervais laughed at her honesty. She might be a penniless social climber but she was no fool.

'And why not, when, with no daughters of her own to overwhelm with such lavish attentions, she had such a charming Goddaughter on whom to bestow a Season in London? She must be delirious with happiness tonight!'

Patricia caught the cynical tone of his words and sighed ruefully. 'You are quite right, Mr Darvill! It is rather overdone, isn't it? But it is fun as well . . . and no-one means all the elaborate things they say and all the compliments they make! It's a sort of game, isn't it?'

He raised an eyebrow and asked with a show of quiet indignation, 'What, even my compliments, Miss Farrington? Am I playing a game also?'

Patricia eyed him honestly, feeling a

warm blush creep over her skin. She wished she could tell him of her game and apologise for its making, but this was not the proper occasion. She should have disabused him of it on her previous meeting, but that hadn't seemed the right place either! Oh, dear! She was just going to have to live with it!

'Yes, you are playing a game, Mr Darvill. You know these people have some regard for you and, maybe from kindness, I don't know, you have chosen to honour my Ball with your presence . . . and I thank you for it, if it eases my acceptance by London's Society.'

'I came to let you know about our mutual friend . . . Jimmy, he tells me he is called. You will be happy to know that he is in residence among my outdoor staff, who are bearing his presence with great fortitude.'

'Oh, I am glad to hear it!' She beamed her pleasure. 'I knew you would not be sorry to have taken him!'

'That remains to be seen, Miss Farrington. I will keep you informed of his progress.' He rose to his feet and bowed briefly, his eyes lingering on hers, wondering at the strange reluctance he felt at departing so soon. 'It has been a pleasure to attend your Ball . . . and I hope you enjoy your Season.'

Patricia watched him depart with mixed feelings. Did he believe her false claim or had he seen though her and was choosing not to refer to it?

6

Although Mr Darvill did not stay to dance, his attentions to Miss Farrington were noted and it was generally agreed that her credentials must be of an impeccable quality for that particular gentleman to pay her such a compliment. Even Lady Sefton, one of the patronesses of Almack's, was moved to assure Lady Hartridge that she would put forward Miss Farrington's name at the forthcoming committee meeting and she was sure that vouchers for Almack's would be hand-delivered within the week.

During the course of the next two weeks, Patricia led a giddy existence of receiving countless invitations to parties, dances, the theatre and a multitude of less formal gatherings. Whenever she and Lady Hartridge ventured out for a drive in the park, they were besieged by admirers stopping to pay her compliments and to extend yet more invitations to a host of pleasurable activities.

During this heady time, she received no less than six proposals of marriage, all of which she graciously declined, knowing that her heart was not engaged by any of the eager, and then woebegone, supplicants. Life was too exciting for her to welcome the sobering effect of becoming engaged so soon in the Season, though she knew she must, if she were to live up to her mother's expectations, accept such an offer before the Season ended.

The proposals were flattering and boosted her confidence but, after hearing that Lady Hartridge had turned down twenty suitors before Lord Hartridge had made his offer, they did not go to Patricia's head.

Her turning down of so many proposals did not go unnoticed however, but Patricia was obliviously unaware that the affairs of her heart were of any interest to society in general, nor that the disappointed young men shared their despair with her other suitors. Word of each rejection was passed along the line of gossip, making her other beaux hopeful that they might be the one who would succeed where others had failed . . . and unintentionally added to the allure of the Season's favourite newcomer.

The refusals also caused a frown of surprise on Mr Darvill's brow. For whom was Miss Farrington holding out? Didn't she dream of marrying someone rich like all the other girls did? He knew for a fact that some of the rejected suitors came from reasonable backgrounds, and whose expectations of wealth, although nowhere matching his own, were nonetheless of notable worth. Surely any one of them would have been a 'catch' for the impecunious Miss Farrington? Could he be mistaken in his belief that she was not the heiress she had claimed to be?

Or, was it a title she was after? There was a smattering of such among the admiring throng that were constantly paying court to Miss Farrington. Maybe he had better warn Jeremy . . . enlighten him to the reality of Miss Farrington's likely prospects? Or was she hoping to attract Lord Hartridge himself when he returned from his wanderings on the continent? He chuckled inwardly at that thought. Good lord! She'd be in for a shock if she had never seen him! A portly, sour-faced grandee if ever there was one! Somehow, he hoped that wasn't Miss Farrington's intention. He didn't like to think of her with someone so unsuited to her.

But neither did he want to see his gullible friend, Jeremy, deceived and beguiled into thinking he might be marrying a fortune . . . for, during his brief visit to Miss Farrington's Ball, he had seen Jeremy's eyes glowering at Miss Farrington's other admirers . . . and believed him to be duly smitten by both a pretty face and an expectation of a fortune.

He went straight to the point when he met Lord Fulford at White's that evening. His friend was engaged in a solitary game of billiards, his brow creased in deep thought. Gervais feared he might, even at this moment, be considering taking the momentous step of asking for Miss Farrington's hand . . . and expecting to be accepted.

Jeremy was titled, of excellent pedigree, handsome and good-natured to boot! All his family lacked was money! But did Miss Farrington know that? Had Lady Hartridge schooled her well? Or did the thought of a title weigh more than wealth with the naïve Miss Farrington?

He sauntered over to his friend's side and drew him aside on the pretext of offering him a pinch of a new blend of snuff he was trying. 'Made the blend myself,' he murmured, flicking open the small gilt box. 'By-the-by, Jeremy, about Miss Farrington. I feel I must . . . '

Jeremy's whole demeanour sagged. 'Oh! You've heard, have you? That was quick! I only asked her this afternoon! Still, I'm not downhearted!'

'Miss Farrington turned you down?'

Jeremy gave a half laugh. 'Caught her on the hop, no doubt! Should have paved the way better! I'll ask her again in a couple of weeks.' He eyed Gervais speculatively. 'I don't suppose you'd care to put in a good word for me, Gerv?'

Gervais raised his eyebrow. 'After that vulgar abbreviation of my name, you suppose quite right, Jeremy!'

He offered further felicitations to his friend but realised that Jeremy wished to drown his sorrows in no other company than his own and Gervais left him to do so, deep in his own thoughts. Hmm! So what exactly was Miss Farrington hoping for?

He had a good mind to keep a close watch on the little baggage and find out exactly what game she was playing, for he knew without doubt that she was playing at something! And, still piqued by her comparison of him to her father, he came to the conclusion that, in order to protect his friend, he must see if he could make Miss Farrington fall in love with him. That would teach her that he was not a fool to be played with! And it would be just retribution for her own foolhardy pretence!

Oh, she would be cast down when she discovered his charade but she would get over it and would return to Lancashire or wherever it was she came from and marry some middle-class merchant or some such . . . and, in years to come, she would regale her numerous offspring and grandchildren with tales of her wonderful Season in London when she was the Belle of every Ball!

Consequently, it seemed to Patricia that everywhere she went over the next week or so, Mr Darvill was sure to be there. Of course, he was a welcome asset to any gathering and Society hostesses were honoured by his presence, even if he had not actually been personally invited.

When, on Patricia's first visit to Almack's, she looked up to see him bowing before her and requesting the pleasure of looking at her dance card, she was so startled she dropped it at his feet. He was wearing a coat the colour of claret with a waistcoat of fine brocade. Dark high-heeled shoes adorned his feet and his stockings were clocked with diamonds. His short dark hair was brushed forward and his eyes danced with merriment, reinforcing Patricia's belief that he was amused by her gaucheness.

Blushing furiously, she watched in some agitation as he wrote his name in two places, convinced he was enjoying her discomfort. When he handed back the card, smiling widely, she was dismayed to see that he had written his name by the first quadrille of the evening, since it was not an easy dance to execute, and a later '*dance a contre*,' commonly known as a country-dance. To hide her confusion, she tilted her head high and met his eyes with a cool composure that belied her true feelings. Let him laugh if he wished. It was nothing to her!

Patricia was thankful that she and Emily had procured patterns of the correct steps of the quadrille and had laboriously practised the figures and changes in their parlour. This poor imitation of the dance had given them adequate skill for their local Assembly Rooms and Patricia hoped it would do so here in this illustrious place.

She later had no memory of the dances before the quadrille but she supposed she must have performed them reasonably well for her enthusiastic partners made no adverse comment. On the contrary, they beamed their pleasure and said they looked forward to the pleasure of dancing with her again later in the evening.

By the time the quadrille was announced, she felt so nervous about it that, even if she hadn't decided to give Mr Darvill a severe let-down by speaking to him as little as was deemed polite, she had to concentrate so much on the steps and keeping to their place in the square formation of four couples that if she had intended to chatter non-stop, she would have found it impossible.

Executing the jettés, chassées and the pas de basque took all her concentration and she noted with a mixture of admiration and pique that Mr Darvill performed the intricate steps with considerable grace. No doubt he had had more practice than she had, she sourly decided.

However, she didn't make any extreme blunders and was relieved to be escorted back to her place when the musicians finished playing with her pride still intact. She curtsied to Mr Darvill's bow and took grateful refuge behind her fan.

Two country-dances followed after that, both of which she knew well and danced with great enjoyment. Algernon claimed her for the cotillion and when the waltz was announced, she was thankful that Almack's patronesses forbade it being danced by any young lady not yet presented at court, although she couldn't help scanning the dancing partners who were allowed on the floor, but Mr Darvill was not among them.

She decided that he had probably regretted marking her card for the next country-dance and had gone on to his club, having made an obligatory appearance at the rooms in King Street . . . and so she was once again taken by surprise when he was suddenly bowing before her once again. This time, she made no error, curtsied nicely before him and laid her hand lightly upon his as he led her to take their place in the set.

She enjoyed dancing and could not remain on her high horse with her partner for long and so, this time, she responded to his conversation and showed great delight when he informed her of Jimmy's progress in his training as a stable lad.

'He has a good 'feel' for horses and will do well if he persists, though he can be a rascal at times,' he informed her as they progressed down the centre of the set.

Before Patricia could ask what he meant, they had parted at the end of the promenade and she had to wait until they met to form part of a 'star' with their hands before she could enquire, 'What does he do?'

'He is my self-appointed shadow,' he told her. 'If I required a page-boy to hold up the tails of my coat, he would apply for the job!'

Patricia laughed aloud at the picture thus described, drawing raised eyebrows from the other couple making up the 'star' and she was forced to confine her mirth to her dancing eyes for the remainder of the dance.

After returning her to her place when the music ceased and making a fine leg as he bowed, she saw Mr Darvill make his adieus to the patronesses and felt some of the sparkle had gone out of the

Assembly Room, though the swift turnover of her partners for the remaining dances left her no time to ponder the fact.

Mr Darvill next turned up with Lord Fulford at a private rout at the home of Lady Isherwood who was launching her twin-daughters on to the marriage mart that Season. They were a pair of giddy girls who laughed and simpered at every comment uttered to them and Patricia couldn't help smiling at the look of patient boredom on Mr Darvill's face when he was partnering first one and then the other in the opening dances. Heaven forbid that she ever put such an expression on his face! However, Lord and Lady Isherwood were well-heeled and the girls were never short of partners.

Patricia refrained from commenting on the sigh of relief Mr Darvill made on claiming her hand for the cotillion. She now had more confidence in her own ability to get through even the most complicated of dances and was noticeably more relaxed with the persistent Mr Darvill. She knew that people had noticed his attentions towards her and Lord Fulford had forcibly expressed his annoyance that his friend should attempt to cut him out of the running so blatantly.

'Don't let him sway your head, Miss Farrington!' he urged her. 'I know for a fact he ain't looking to get riveted!'

His words echoed what she had overheard Mr Darvill himself declare on their first meeting and she responded lightly that she had no expectations in that quarter . . . but, in the privacy of her bedroom, she wondered how true her words had been. What would she do if he proved to have had a change of heart and presented himself, hat in hand, to make her an offer?

In all truth, she could not envisage it happening. She was a 'novelty newcomer' . . . nothing more. But his attentions were very flattering and raised her credibility among the *haut ton.*

When a party of a dozen or so young people visited Bullock's Museum in Piccadilly, Mr Darvill was suddenly at Patricia's side, much to her confusion, for the sight of the preserved rhinos, elephants and giraffes had caused her to exclaim aloud at in a way that her younger sister, Meg, might have done.

'There are many more exotic animals on exhibit, Miss Farrington,' he murmured, gently taking hold of her elbow and guiding her into the next room, all the while commenting on the wonders to be seen as they passed them by.

'Why, th . . . thank you, Mr Darvill,' she stammered, glancing around hoping some of her party would rescue her from this somewhat daunting man. However, his instruction was so interesting that she found herself willingly following his progress from exhibit to exhibit and, when others joined them, forming a small group, she found herself relaxing in his presence.

At the end of that visit, Mr Darvill found himself included in the future plans to visit the Astley's Amphitheatre, where the crowds were treated to spectacular acts of horsemanship and acrobatic riding; and the Tower of London, where visitors could see Traitor's Gate and the Bloody Tower; the crown jewels; and artefacts dating from the time of King John.

The added appeal for the young people was the menagerie in the Lion Tower, where, for the admission price of one shilling, they were shown around the yard by the keeper who could tell his enraptured audience about the wild animals caged there, which included several lions, tigers, leopards, a panther and a wolf.

Some of the young men at first viewed Mr Darvill's presence with glowering, dark looks but when Miss Farrington continued to divide her time and attention between them all, they ceased to regard him as a serious rival and since he was known to be flush with funds and didn't seem to mind putting his hand into his pocket, they very soon decided he was a bang-up cove.

Street Fairs were all the fashion and offered a wide range of attractions. At one such event, Patricia was astonished to see a fire-eating lady and was so convinced that she was about to witness that lady's sudden demise, she hurriedly turned away and buried her face in the nearest male chest.

It was a strange sensation to be held so close and to feel the strength of the masculine body standing firmly against her. The 'touch' of the cloth was different and the pleasant pine-scented fragrance made her feel somewhat heady. It was an agreeable sensation and it was only her innate sense of decorum that made her draw back slightly, when, to her utter mortification, she found her 'protector' to be none other than Mr Darvill.

'See, all is well, Miss Farrington,' he murmured as the feat was drawn to its conclusion and he turned her around to see the 'fire-eater' making her triumphant bow to the applauding crowd.

'Oh! I apologise, sir! I am not usually so timid,' she hurriedly excused herself, trying to draw further away.

Gervais smiled warmly; his role as 'protector' had not been unpleasant. 'The performers intend to thrill and frighten their audience,' he assured her. 'Your reaction has made her day. See how she beams at you.'

The woman, dressed in oriental costume, was indeed smiling her way and Patricia smilingly nodded her head towards her to acknowledge the success of her act. 'Though I am sure I don't know how she does it!' she exclaimed as Gervais led her away.

'That is her 'secret',' Gervais murmured in her ear, the warmth of his breath sending a tingling sensation around Patricia's body. 'Come, there is plenty more to see.'

There were puppets, magicians, wire-walkers, and a small prize-fighting ring where the young men were extolled to come and try their strength against the well-muscled, bronze-skinned man.

When a roughly clad young man went boldly forward, stripping off his jacket, some of the young ladies squealed in apprehension but Patricia reckoned the young man must know what he was up against and the proceeding 'fight' seemed very tame to her.

'I think that was fixed beforehand,' she commented, surprised to find Mr Darvill still at her side.

'Much of what goes on here is for 'show',' he agreed, 'but they have an appreciative audience who are willing to toss a few pennies in the box for the pleasure of being thrilled or astonished.'

They rounded a corner to see a man with a large brown bear anchored to the ground by a stout chain. The bear was painfully thin, its fur mangy and its eyes lacking any lustre. Red sores showed around its ankle where the metal cuff chafed at his skin. A boy at the man's side played music with a squeeze box whilst the man prodded the bear's legs with a long stick.

'Roll up! Roll up to see the only

dancing bear in England!'

'Oh! But that's cruel!' Patricia declared, immediately disengaging herself from Mr Darvill's arm and striding forward to remonstrate with the unkempt man. 'How dare you so ill-treat that poor animal?' she cried passionately. 'He needs care and attention! Not . . . not to be so publicly displayed!'

'Shove off, missy!' the man growled at her.

'Indeed, I will not! You ought to be prosecuted for such cruelty! Mr Darvill, tell this man . . . '

'Shove off, the pair o' yer!' the man repeated, raising his fist and shaking it very near to Patricia's face. 'Or I'll shove yer off meself!'

Gervais caught hold of Patricia's arm and drew her back towards him, putting himself between her and the threatening gesture of the man. He faced the man coolly. 'I would advise you not to threaten this young lady,' he said in level tones.

'An' what'll yer do if I don't?' the

man sneered. He was a large man and his leering face was almost on a level with Gervais's own.

Gervais, conscious of the onlookers now glancing their way . . . and of the other ladies in their own party who were now drawing near to see what the commotion was about, did not wish to prolong the encounter. Making use of the extra inches of height he had over the man, he drawled, 'Let us say you would find yourself greatly incommoded!' deliberately using language above the man's intelligence.

The man's eyes flickered nervously from side to side, as if looking for some dire form of retribution about to befall him. 'Aye, well,' he muttered, 'just shove off like I said . . . and we'll say no more about it, eh?'

Gervais gave him a curt nod and the man withdrew a pace or two. Gervais took a firm hold of Patricia's elbow and guided her in the direction of their party.

'But it is so cruel!' Patricia repeated.

'That poor bear! Did you see the state of it? It isn't meant to dance for our enjoyment! May I not inform that man of his duty to one of God's creatures?'

'And what then?' Gervais asked gently.

'Why, I will tell him to set it free!' Patricia exclaimed.

Gervais spread his free hand wide. 'Where? Here in the midst of the city?'

Patricia was silenced for a moment.

'Well . . . no. I can see that that is not possible,' she grudgingly allowed after some thought, 'but there must be somewhere it could be taken.' Her eyes suddenly lit up and she took hold of his arm with both of her hands. 'I know! Mr Darvill, we could buy it . . . as long as it doesn't cost too much . . . and you could . . . '

Gervais stopped her there.

'No, Miss Farrington! You have persuaded me to take an extra servant into my household, but I refuse to attempt to accommodate a dancing bear! Jimmy has done enough to put

111

my household into some disarray but I think a dancing bear would persuade most of my servants that I have lost my reason and hand in their notices forthwith!'

His voice was firm but not unkind and Patricia felt emboldened to entreat him further. 'I just thought you might find a better place for it,' she said in a quiet voice, 'like with the wild animals at the Tower of London. They didn't seem to be too badly treated, though I expect any sort of imprisonment is unpleasant for them.'

A tiny tear was trickling down Miss Farrington's cheek and Gervais gently wiped it away with the pad of his thumb as he regarded her sombre face. 'You have a tender heart,' he said softly, 'but you cannot cure the whole world of its ills.' In most other young ladies of his acquaintance, he would suspect that tear to be false . . . squeezed out in the hope of some gain for themselves, not for a mangy old bear that seemed not long for this world. 'I tell you what I will do. I will approach the keepers at the Tower Zoo and, if they say they can accommodate a bear, I will find this man again tomorrow and purchase his bear for you. How does that take you?'

Patricia's eyes lit up. 'Oh, that is really . . . ' She was lost for words.

Gervais tucked her hand into the bend of his arm. 'And in return, I must ask for some . . . recompense.'

Patricia halted and looked at him in some alarm. 'Recompense?'

He smiled, his eyes twinkling at her dismay. 'Yes, I must ask that you will come driving with me tomorrow, in the afternoon of course, as I will be somewhat busy in the morning! It would give me great pleasure,' he added, when she continued to stare disbelievingly at him.

Patricia was surprised by this invitation. Although he had singled her out on outings such as this, he hadn't before invited her individually to any place of entertainment.

'J . . . just me?' she faltered.

Gervais smiled. 'I'm afraid I don't possess a carriage large enough to accommodate all your friends!'

'Oh. Then I suppose I must . . . accept,' she replied less graciously than she ought, but her mind felt paralysed. Did he, even yet, intend to challenge her claim to be an heiress? Was she never to be allowed to forget that momentary lapse from her honest upbringing?

7

However, when Patricia wondered aloud to Lady Hartridge if maybe she ought to decline the invitation . . . though she didn't apprise Lady Hartridge for her reason 'why' . . . Lady Hartridge was effusive in encouraging her otherwise.

'My dear, of course you must accept! Such an honour! Such a compliment! Though I owe that I never expected you to catch the eye of someone quite so eligible! He is a non-pareil in every way! A 'Corinthian'! What good fortune for you if he has at long last decided he must choose a wife! Of course, it might just be that he feels an obligation to you, meeting you, as he did, on your journey here . . . or, of course, he might just be 'playing' with your affections.'

'On the other hand, you have 'taken' so well and have shown yourself to be almost indifferent to him, it has probably dented his pride a little. But, if that is so, you must use a little artifice! Tease him a little! Play him on a hook and line! Why, I used to tease thus my dear Hartridge all the time until he vowed he would die of a broken heart if I did not take pity on him and become his betrothed!'

Patricia was not reassured. 'Ma'am, I have no plans to tease Mr Darvill! Nor to play him on a hook and line! I am sure he is just showing some . . . friendliness . . . towards me! Nothing more than that. Why, the mere thought of 'teasing' him makes me quail!'

'Nonsense! A pretty girl like you holds all the aces! Kitty must accompany you, of course, for it would be considered very 'fast' of you to drive unaccompanied. And you must carry that pretty little parasol I gave you yesterday.'

And so at a quarter to five on the following afternoon, dressed in a fetching carriage gown of darkest red and a matching poke bonnet trimmed with flowers and lace, Patricia welcomed Mr Darvill with a modest curtsey and descended the front steps into Duke Street with her hand resting lightly on his arm, with Kitty just a few paces behind.

Her initial wariness was dispelled when she saw that Mr Darvill had come in his curricle drawn by two matching bays and intended her to sit by his side on the driving seat. Kitty was assigned to the rear rumble seat along with Mr Darvill's groom, which by no means displeased her maid if her pleased grin was anything to go by.

'Did you rescue the bear, Mr Darvill?' Patricia asked once his steeds were high-stepping their way along Grosvenor Street on the way to Hyde Park.

Mr Darvill briefly took his eyes from the road ahead and smiled at the intensity of her expression. 'I have made arrangements for it to be housed in the Tower menagerie, though not yet to be put on display owing to its poor condition. Its present owner has promised to deliver it there tomorrow morning, when he will be given suitable recompense.'

'I wonder what he will do after that?' Patricia asked, suddenly feeling concerned for the man's welfare. 'I wonder if he has a family to support? Do you think he will have an alternative way to make a living?'

'He will probably procure another bear to train,' Mr Darvill said dryly.

Patricia was horrified. 'But he isn't fit to keep an animal!' she exclaimed. 'We must stop him! There must be something else he can do!'

Gervais glanced down at the puckered frown on her face. 'I'm sure you will think of something, Miss Farrington.'

'It will have to be something manual, I think,' she responded thoughtfully. 'I shouldn't think he has had much education.'

'Probably none at all.'

She nodded sagely. 'Probably not.

Life is very tough for the poor, especially in a city.'

He glanced at her again, touched by her sincerity. 'You really care, don't you, Miss Farrington?'

She looked at him carefully, seeking for some sign of derision in his expression, but finding none. 'Papa says it is our duty to bear the burdens of others as we walk our pilgrim way. We should all use what we have to help those who have nothing, but in the city there is so much poverty it is difficult to know where to start.'

Mr Darvill turned away as she spoke in order to concentrate on tooling his vehicle through the gateway to Hyde Park on to Rotten Row, an avenue that encircled the entire Park and which was already much crowded by ladies promenading in their most fetching gowns and dandies 'on the strut', openly ogling the ladies and keeping a careful eye on the other bucks in case any outdid them in sporting the latest fashion.

'Especially when you see all of this?' Mr Darvill suggested.

Patricia glanced about her. She knew it was the place to be between five o'clock and six in the afternoon. People recognised her and, of course, her companion. Patricia knew she was the envy of those of her own age with aspirations to cut a dash.

Yet what did it all mean? Wasn't it all just a thin veneer of gaiety that attempted to conceal the harsher realities of life under its gilt and glitter? Suddenly, she wasn't sure that she wanted to be a part of it. She was more at home in her own village where, in many small ways, her mama and papa did make a difference in the lives of others.

Mr Darvill glanced at her pensive face and his heart contracted.

'Our talk has saddened you,' he said. 'I hadn't meant it to do so.'

She shook her head. 'It isn't anything you have said. I suddenly thought of home and thought how much more meaningful everything is there. And yet I am enjoying all of this. It is exciting to be part of London's Society and to find myself accepted by the *haut ton*. I never expected . . . ' She gave a short laugh. 'I am not so bird-witted as to suppose that it is on my account, of course, so I will not let it go to my head or give me ideas above myself, but it makes me wonder why I am here and what life will be like when I return home. Will it make me critical of all that I have loved at home?'

'I think you will take whatever you have learned from your time in London and use it to better the conditions and lives of others,' Mr Darvill said quietly. 'But to do that properly, you need to enjoy what you are experiencing here so that you will have vitality and, possibly, the means by which to help others.'

'Do you think so?' she asked earnestly.

'I do. You are young, Miss Farrington. As yet you have no means of helping others . . . and yet you have rescued Jimmy from a life of crime, a bear from ill-treatment and, now, a veritable rogue who might or might not be willing to accept some sort of manual labour on one of my estates.'

'Oh!' Her face brightened. She had to admit that she was surprised by his benevolence towards her acts of philanthropy and added blithely, 'Do you intend to offer the bear's trainer a job?'

'Dare I do aught else?' he asked in mock surprise. 'But this is the last time, Miss Farrington! I will take on no more of your waifs, strays or vagabonds, do you hear?' At least, not yet, he echoed in his heart, strangely moved by the intensity of her concern for others. 'Now, to change the subject, do you know how this avenue became known as Rotten Row?'

He smiled as her brow furrowed and her lips pursed in thought. Such enticing lips, he couldn't help thinking.

'Rotten Row?' she repeated slowly, her intention diverted by the question.

'It must be something that sounds like something else,' she surmised, 'for this is such a beautiful place here in the midst of the city. Hmm, French has always been the courtly language, so something French, perhaps?'

Gervais gave a slight nod of assent. 'That is quite right, Miss Farrington. Very astute of you.'

Patricia wondered if he were deriding her knowledge and hastened to defend her position. 'Papa is of the belief that girls benefit from education just as much as boys and so he insisted that we all learned our lessons,' she said sharply, adding ruefully, 'And now, I expect you think I am nothing but a blue-stocking, Mr Darvill!'

'By no means, Miss Farrington. Being such a dull character would never be an accusation levelled at you. Now, *Route du Roi* . . . does that help?'

'Hmm, *Route du Roi*? The way of the king? So, which king was that? One of the Stuarts, perhaps?'

Gervais couldn't help laughing as she

turned her pouting lips towards him. 'Maybe you are a blue-stocking after all, Miss Farrington!' he teased, his eyes twinkling down at her upturned face. 'You are close. It was William III. He had to regularly make his way from Kensington Palace to St James's so he ordered the route of his travel to be lit by three hundred oil lamps. So, it became known as the 'route du roi', soon to be mutated into 'rotten row' in the common parlance. Now, the history lesson is over . . . and another sort about to begin!'

He was enjoying himself and grinned at her quizzical expression. 'Do you drive at all, Miss Farrington?'

'A little,' she allowed, smiling up at him, now totally relaxed. 'Of course we only have a small gig of our own and I drive that quite a lot but my cousin, Harry, has taught me to drive his barouche and reckons that I am up to the mark!'

Hmm, so she had a cousin and brothers, did she? Gervais mused, mentally storing these snippets of information.

'Then, close your parasol and hand it to your maid and allow me to transfer the reins into your hands, Miss Farrington, and we'll see how 'up to the mark' you are!'

She deftly took the reins from his hands and, although he let his hands linger over hers for a short while, he was soon able to sit back and relax as she drove his pair with more than adequate skill and accomplishment around the perimeter of Hyde Park.

Whatever he had expected to feel when he began this 'charade', he knew the time spent in Miss Farrington's presence had somehow surpassed his expectations. There was a swell of contentment deep within him . . . and, for once in his life, he didn't know what the outcome would be.

Although Patricia was not the first woman to drive a carriage along Rotten Row, it wasn't an everyday occurrence and her feat did not go unnoticed but although she did no more than briefly nod to her acknowledgement of raised hats, he knew from her heightened colour and bright eyes that she was not unaware of the admiration that followed her progress.

Ha! He was enjoying this! And he wanted it to continue.

'Shall we walk around the lake?' he suggested, seeing it just ahead of them.

Patricia reined the horses to a standstill and handed the reins to the groom who had leaped from the rear seat as soon as the vehicle stopped. Gervais leaped down from the driving seat and hurried around the back of the curricle to assist Miss Farrington descend.

Patricia wished she could leap down with the same dignity as her companion but knew that the skirts of her carriage dress would not allow such hoydenish behaviour, so she waited until Mr Darvill was at her side. She was partly afraid to touch this man — he disturbed her in a way she didn't quite understand.

All she knew was that his nearness caused her heart to flutter erratically, especially as she leaned towards him and placed her hands upon his shoulders, allowing him to take hold of her around her waist and lift her down.

For a moment, she was pressed against him and, although he towered above her, he bent his head down and their faces almost touched. She sensed a quickening of his breath and her own breath caught in her throat. For an insane moment, she longed to reach up and trace her fingertips down his cheek and maybe touch his lips . . . and it seemed as though her heart stopped beating at the thought.

How would he respond? Her lips tingled and parted slightly . . . and, for a fleeting moment, she believed he was going to caress her lips with his, but the bays stirred restlessly, causing the curricle to move behind her and she involuntarily stepped away a little to regain her balance and the moment passed.

She didn't know how shaken Gervais was. He had been taken completely by surprise by his reaction when he lifted Miss Farrington down. He was used to sophisticated women; women with some experience; women who wouldn't have hesitated to seize the moment for an illicit caress . . . and he had almost forgotten that this girl was untouched as his lips had moved instinctively to claim that enticing rosy-pink, slightly parted mouth no more than an inch or so away from his. His lips felt cheated, but he was relieved that he hadn't succumbed to the temptation.

She trusted him and he had almost betrayed that trust. He also knew a sense of disappointment. If he had kissed her in so public a place, he would have been compelled to offer for her hand, an offer that would surely have been accepted — and he was surprised to realise that that would not have dismayed him — although that was not a part of his plan.

He swiftly suppressed such wayward

thoughts and, whilst Miss Farrington was occupied in gathering up the train of her carriage dress, he composed his features and offered her his arm. 'Come, let us walk.'

Patricia's emotions were whirling by the time she was delivered back into Lady Hartridge's safe keeping. Contrary to her expectations, she had thoroughly enjoyed her outing with Mr Darvill and supposed that he had enjoyed it also, since he had asked Lady Hartridge's permission to repeat the exercise and had invited her to ride with him in two days time.

She didn't have much time to dwell upon the afternoon as she had an engagement with Algernon Albright that evening, along with a party of eight other young people and their chaperones, to visit the theatre in Drury Lane. Kitty hurriedly divested her of her carriage dress, washed her skin with rose-scented water, attired her in her evening gown and re-dressed her hair.

The play enthralled her but she

found the constant loud conversations among the audience, especially those in the pit, quite distracting and wondered how the actors and actresses managed to concentrate on their lines. Some of the bolder members of the audience, even some in boxes such as her party, called across the auditorium to their acquaintances and there were gentlemen openly ogling ladies in not their own parties through their quizzing glasses.

Sometimes, she knew those glasses were trained upon her and although she felt it quite unladylike to return the scrutiny, she couldn't help wondering who some of them were. She waited until the interval before she glanced around the auditorium to see if she could identify anyone.

Under the cover of glancing around and talking to members of her party, her eyes swept over the other boxes and she knew that Mr Darvill was not present. Although she felt she would have liked to have seen him again, she decided she was glad he was not there, for she knew she would have felt quite jealous of any female he might have escorted . . . though she doubted if he would suffer the same pangs if he had witnessed Algernon's solicitous attentions to her.

How different were her thoughts about the two men. One amused her by his extravagant compliments and over-lavish praises of her beauty and accomplishments, but left her heart untouched . . . whilst merely thinking of the other made her heart beat a little faster and sent strange sensations coursing through her body.

She could almost hear her mama's voice saying, 'It will only end in tears!'

8

The activities planned for the next few days left little time for Patricia to dwell upon the capricious nature of her heart, nor to find the space of time to allow her to accept the invitation to go riding in Hyde Park with Mr Darvill, although a date was fixed for the following week.

A lively group of young people visited the Pantheon Bazaar, followed by fruit ices in Gunter's; Sir Charles Overton took a small party to visit the Florida Gardens; and, another day, when the sun shone brightly, four carriages drove to Richmond Hill. The ladies travelled in carriages with their chaperones with the young men on horseback. Mr Darvill was among the latter and he cut a fine figure astride his black stallion.

An enjoyable half hour was spent in light banter, culminating in a discussion about the current political situation and whether or not it was right that individual MPs were free to move between the parties and vote according to their conscience on any particular issue or should a Whig be always a Whig and a Tory a Tory, and should the Prince Regent have as much influence as if he were indeed king of the realm?

Patricia was surprised by how little most of the other young women contributed to the discussion and wondered if it were because they had never been given the opportunity to consider such issues, or was it that they truly had no interest. When she voiced this thought, she discovered that it was mainly the latter and the consensus of opinion seemed to be that women did not have sufficient brain power to have any lasting interest in matters of state.

'And since women will never have the right to vote on any issue,' Freddie Maynard pointed out, 'there is little point in any of you worrying your pretty little heads about such matters. Leave it to us men! You will all soon have husbands to do your thinking for you.'

Patricia almost exploded and rounded upon him indignantly. 'No man will ever do my thinking for me, I can assure you!' A statement which shocked the chaperones and most of the young women, although a few of the young bucks applauded her.

Later, back at home, Lady Hartridge reproved her for being so outspoken, 'For you will find most young men greatly put off by too much boldness in a young lady,' she pointed out. 'I hope this doesn't bring an end to the proposals of marriage you have been receiving!'

Patricia didn't want to return home as a failure and hoped she hadn't been too hasty in turning down the earlier proposals. She wasn't in love with any of them . . . and the one who did touch her heart was out of her reach!

However, the very next day, Lady Hartridge's fears were proved ground-less. It rained all morning and Lady

Hartridge felt compelled to cancel a planned visit to the shops in Oxford Street in the afternoon. 'Everywhere will be extremely wet. Much better to have a quiet afternoon and do some quiet sewing instead.'

Patricia willingly fell in with the new plan, for, to tell the truth, the money her Uncle William had given to her was nearly all spent and there was little pleasure in shopping when you had little money to spend. After a light luncheon, Lady Hartridge decided to retire to her boudoir for a rest and Patricia, with only Kitty in attendance, happily added a few stitches to the tapestry she had started.

At two o'clock, Kettering tapped on the door of the drawing room and entered with a bow. Patricia knew he was about to announce a visitor and her heart leaped. Had Mr Darvill come to call?

'Mr Albright wishes to know if you are home, Miss Farrington.'

'Oh.'

She was disappointed by the name but thankful to see a friendly face . . . unless he had come to chide her for her very unfeminine views! Kitty rose from her seat beside her and retired to a seat by the window where she could watch the passers-by.

When Algernon Albright strode into the room and made an elaborate bow, it soon became obvious that he had something other than Patricia's outspokenness on his mind. He seemed quite nervous and after making a few faltering opening pleasantries, he began to pace up and down in front of the sofa where Patricia was seated.

'Oh, do come and sit down, Algernon!' she bade him. 'I feel quite dizzy watching you pace back and forth!'

Instead of seating himself, Algernon dropped on to one knee before her and seized hold of her hand. 'Miss Farrington! Patricia! May I call you by your name . . . for I say it over and over to myself at night? It is like honey on my lips!'

Patricia's heart sank. She felt she knew what was coming and didn't know how to stop him without seeming impolite.

He took her silence as agreement to use her forename and said it again. 'Patricia! You must know how I feel about you, and I thought you were magnificent yesterday! You are a girl in a million and I do so hope you will do me the honour of agreeing to become my wife!'

Patricia tried to extricate her hand from his grip but he was holding it too firmly.

'Oh, Algernon, I do like you and consider you to be my friend but . . . '

'Oh, don't say it, please, I beg you! You mustn't fear that I will be a heavy-handed husband! You will find I am in agreement that wives should not be down-trodden . . . and I am not influenced by your expectations of great fortune, Miss Farrington. Though of course, one can never have too much money, can one? But, happily, I have plenty of my own, so you must know that it is you I have fallen in love with!'

'My fortune?' Patricia echoed hollowly.

'Why, yes . . . I mean, no, it's not your fortune, but everyone is talking about it . . . though I did hear that you don't want it to be so, but you know how it is!'

Patricia was hardly aware of his babbling. Her mind felt numb. Everyone thought she was an heiress! But she had only said it in pique to Mr Darvill and Lord Fulford . . . and she had told them not to spread it around. How had it happened? Her only concern had been that Mr Darvill might have believed her and she had had no inkling that anyone else might be under the same misapprehension. Oh, dear! One or both of them must have spoken of her declared expectations! Oh, how could they!

'So, can you give me hope, Miss Farrington?' Algernon implored, not sure how to take her stricken expression.

'Oh! No, no! I can't! I can't possibly!'

Oh! Patricia clasped her hand to her mouth as she realised the enormity of what she had done! For, if everyone thought she was heiress to a fortune, as soon as she accepted any proposal, she would have to admit to her deception and she would be exposed as a fortune huntress and deceiver, and its admission would make her feel compelled to tell Lady Hartridge of her deception before anyone did so . . . and that good lady would be so disgusted by her unchristian behaviour, that she would demand her instant return to her home . . . and that would disappoint her mama . . . and disgust her papa . . . and that was more than she could bear to think about! In her agitation, she was twisting her hands together in her lap, twisting the folds of her muslin gown.

And what of Mr Darvill? He must have believed her! How could she tell him that she was penniless and ever expected to remain so? He would despise her for evermore!

'Patricia? Miss Farrington?' Algernon hesitantly faltered. 'Is anything amiss? I did not expect my offer to have such a devastating effect upon you. Can I get you anything? Your smelling salts, perhaps? Your maid?' looking hopefully towards Kitty, who had dropped all pretence of sewing and was already rising to her feet.

Patricia had forgotten Kitty's presence. Oh, this was all too embarrassing . . . for Algernon, as well as herself! She fluttered her left hand at her throat. 'Water . . . a glass of water, Kitty. That is all I need.'

'Or something a little stronger?' Algernon suggested, rising to his feet, looking as if he wanted nothing other than to make a hurried exit from the room.

'No, just water, Kitty. Thank you.'

She knew she had to end this embarrassing interview without delay and, although she felt like burying her face in her hands to hide the shame she felt, she tried to compose her chaotic thoughts and make as polite a refusal as she was able.

'Algernon . . . Mr Albright, I must thank you for your kind offer. I . . . I am . . . honoured, but it is impossible for me to accept.'

'Oh, do not say so, Miss Farrington! I thought you must know how I felt! You seemed to accept my advances.'

'I'm sorry. I think of you as one of my brothers!'

'Your brothers? I do not want you as a sister — I want you as my wife!'

'Oh, Algernon!'

He looked so woebegone that she made the mistake of rising to her feet, whereupon Algernon seized hold of her hand again. 'I will wait, give you time to reconsider! Do give me some hope, Miss Farrington!'

'No, no! I cannot! I'm sorry.' The last two words were quietly spoken and, as she uttered them, a quiet, apologetic cough came from the doorway, drawing the attention of them both. It was Mr Darvill.

'Oh!'

Patricia hastily pulled her hand from Algernon's grasp and both hands rose to flutter against her hot cheeks and Algernon stepped to one side, evidently disconcerted to have the finale of his rejection in public view.

Mr Darvill was regarding them quite sternly. However, he made his bow, murmuring, 'Your servant, Miss Farrington,' and nodding curtly to Algernon. 'Mr Albright.'

His right eyebrow rose in that cynical gesture that was already familiar to Patricia and her heart quailed within her. She bobbed a quick curtsey, wishing she could sink right into the floor.

'I'm sorry. Have I interrupted something? Only I heard what seemed like a cry of distress,' Mr Darvill murmured.

'Oh! No . . . no!' Patricia stammered. 'Mr Albright is . . . '

'I was about to take my leave, sir!' Algernon said curtly, his face changing rapidly from white to red and back again as he made a stiff, formal bow. 'Miss Farrington.' He bowed again, less curtly, though more abruptly than he might have wished and swiftly made his exit, leaving Patricia alone with his rival, for that is what he was convinced was the cause of this rejection.

Gervais felt a little at a loss what to say. It was obvious what the nature of Mr Albright's visit had been . . . and it's outcome . . . and, whilst he could do nothing to soothe the wounds of Mr Albright, he could hope to dispel the distress and guilt that Miss Farrington was displaying upon her expressive face.

His heart softened . . . for all her present deception, she was no practised deceiver! Her every thought was transmitted in her facial features! In what manner had that young buck made his proposal to her that had distressed her so? Or, had she wanted to accept him and had disclosed the truth of her situation to him — and then been rejected? As much as the outcome satisfied him, the manner of its happening did not. She looked so distressed that he longed to enfold her in his arms and tell her that everything would be all right, but he couldn't.

'I am sorry. I had no intention of interrupting a private conversation,' he said gently. 'I expected to find your maid with you. Do you require her to be summoned?'

Patricia's mouth felt dry and her hoarseness was genuine when she croaked, 'My maid has gone to fetch me a glass of water, thank you.'

Mr Darvill's presence . . . and the knowledge of the question she must put to him . . . was making her legs feel as if they were about to fail her and she indicated a nearby chair. 'Would you care to be seated, sir?'

Without waiting to see if he did so, she sank down on to the sofa, her heart and stomach fluttering so wildly she felt as if she might faint — though she despised weak females who took refuge in swooning when problems asserted themselves — as they certainly did now! She would have to tell him! She would have to admit to her deception! No matter what the cost!

Gervais hesitated. He would rather have asked Kettering to request Lady Hartridge to join them, but he acceded to Miss Farrington's request and, flicking back the tails of his coat, he seated himself on the upright chair.

Patricia swallowed hard. She had to say it! There was no point in delaying her question any further, though her brain was finding it difficult to select the proper words. 'Mr Darvill,' she faltered, 'I must ask . . . that is, I need to know . . . have you, er, spoken to anyone about . . . what I said the first time we met?'

Ha! The truth was going to be disclosed at last, was it? And not before time! However, he needed to be sure he wasn't mistaking her intent, and why would he make it too easy for her, the little minx? He furrowed his forehead. 'What are you referring to, Miss Farrington?'

'You know, my . . . er . . . expectations of in . . . inheriting from my m . . . many uncles,' she stammered, her cheeks blushing profusely.

'Ah, yes! I recall! Your 'fabulous fortune'!' He smiled. 'No, I haven't discussed it with anyone, since you especially expressed that to be your wish. I cannot say the same for Lord Fulford, of course, but he was there when you made us privy to your secret.'

'Then, it is he who has spread the rumours?' she said in a tiny voice.

'Rumours?'

'You must have heard them! Algernon informs me that everyone is talking about it!'

'Ah, yes! I suppose they are! But you mustn't blame Lord Fulford too much. I am sure he had no intention of telling everyone, but these things have a way of leaking out, you know, and such rumours lose nothing in the retelling. Society can be quite relentless in seeking out anyone's secrets . . . and you have made such a hit with society, you know!'

'But I didn't want to . . . not in that way! Oh, why didn't you squash the rumours? You knew I didn't intend it to be broadcast about!'

His eyes narrowed a little. Was she still hoping to evade admitting the truth? Oh, how he longed that she might trust him!

'I wasn't totally sure what your intention was, Miss Farrington. Sometimes ladies have a habit of saying one thing and yet meaning something quite different!'

'Well, I don't!' she snapped indignantly.

He raised an eyebrow. 'Don't you?'

'No! That is . . . not usually. I just thought . . . '

Oh, why had she done it? And then she had compounded the lie by not renouncing it the next time she met him! She should have told him that it was all untrue; that she had only pretended to be an heiress because she had overheard him deploring scheming women who pursued him for his fortune.

And now he was regarding her with such a ... well, really, a strange expression ... and she wasn't quite sure what it signified. It wasn't the expression she had expected to see upon his face. She had expected to see derision, loathing, perhaps ... whereas he seemed almost tender! She was suddenly confused. Maybe he still didn't realise that she had not been speaking the truth! Did he think her discomfort was simply because everyone knew about her supposed fortune?

Oh, dear! That meant she still had to disabuse him, and then he would despise her!

She clasped her hands together in her lap and tilted her chin high. She had better get it over with!

'Mr Darvill, I must tell you ... '

'Here we are, miss!' Kitty's voice interrupted her confession as she bounced into the drawing room with a tray holding a jug of water and a glass. 'I'm sorry I took so long but Mrs Wilkinson thought you might like a fresh lemon squeezed into it and . . . Ooh, I'm sorry, miss! Sorry, Mr Darvill! I didn't realise you had company, miss! Ooh! I'll just put the tray here and pour you a glass, shall I?'

Kitty did as she said and then scuttled across the room to resume her role of chaperone.

Patricia's mouth dried up completely. There was no way she could make her admission now! She couldn't bear to be so shamed in front of her maid! She looked with silent appeal at Mr Darvill, hoping he wouldn't insist that she completed her sentence.

He didn't. He rose to his feet and bowed before her.

'I'm afraid I must leave you for the time being, Miss Farrington. I came to tell you that I will be unable to honour my intention of taking you riding in a few days time as I will be absent from town for a few days.'

Her heart sank. Did he know the truth, after all? Was this his way of saying that he would have nothing more to do with her? Maybe that was for the best, though it grieved her deeply to acknowledge it. Dismayed by his statement, she rose to bob the obligatory curtsey.

He seemed as though he were about to say more, but, instead, repeated his bow and departed. Just before he gently closed the door behind him, she heard Kettering say, 'Lady Hartridge will receive you in the salon, Mr Darvill, if you will come this way.'

She stared at the closed door. Her game was up! Mr Darvill was about to denounce her!

9

For the next few days Patricia lived in a state of anxiety, waiting for due retribution to fall upon her. So unlike her usual cheerful self did she appear that Lady Hartridge was convinced that she was sickening for something. She cancelled all of Patricia's engagements for the immediate future and summoned her physician.

Patricia felt she was once more caught up in an act of deception. It made her so miserable she was unable to put any spark of life in her being. The physician pronounced that she was suffering from over-excitement caused by her hectic social engagements and needed rest and quiet for a few days, fortified by some good broth and other easy-to-digest delicacies.

All the time, she was expecting Lady Hartridge to challenge her about her false claim to riches and for that good lady to send her packing. After two days of lying in bed and another two days reclining on the sofa with no appetite at all for food, not even the delicacies that Mrs Wilkins made especially for her, Patricia decided to bring her indiscreet behaviour into the open and, pale of face and shaking inwardly, she summoned her feeble courage.

She and Lady Hartridge were seated in the drawing room, both with their stitching to hand, although neither of them had made even one new stitch since they were both lost in thought . . . Lady Hartridge happily so, but Patricia desperately unhappy.

Lady Hartridge was the first to break the silence. She smiled indulgently at Patricia. 'Ah, my dear! You are missing Mr Darvill, aren't you? But don't you fret yourself. He may be even now talking to your mama and papa and will be back before you know it!'

Patricia stared at her aghast. 'Talking to Mama and Papa?' she echoed. Her whole body froze. This was much worse than she had feared. Oh! He must be so disgusted with her that he felt compelled to denounce her to her parents! They would be devastated! 'How . . . how did he know where I live?' she faltered.

'Why, I told him, of course! Oh, such an honour, my dear! Although not entirely unexpected, as I think I mentioned to you the other day!'

Patricia could hardly compose her thoughts. Lady Hartridge had completely misconstrued Mr Darvill's intentions. She must put her right immediately. 'It's not what you think,' she began, determined to make her dreadful confession. 'The worry of it has been making me feel quite ill. I fear I have behaved a little indiscreetly and Mr Darvill . . . '

'My dear! My dear! Say no more!' Lady Hartridge beamed at her. 'I know exactly why Mr Darvill has gone to see your parents, for he told me so himself . . . though he requested that I did speak of it to you before his return!

However, since you have spoken of it yourself, I do not see that I have betrayed his confidence! As for your being indiscreet, I am sure a little hand-holding and allowing Mr Darvill to whisper 'sweet-nothings' in your ear is not too dreadful an indiscretion. I allowed just the same with my dear Hartridge and have never had a moment's worry about it!'

'No, no! You don't understand! Mr Darvill has gone to tell Mama and Papa that I . . . '

' . . . have agreed to him asking for their permission to pay court to you! I know, my dear! And, although you are a sly little minx for not telling me so, I forgive you! Oh, the marvel of it! I never expected you to do so well, but there we are! Cupid's little darts will find their mark!'

There seemed to be a buzzing sound in Patricia's ears and Lady Hartridge's face was looming and receding before her eyes. It was worse than she had thought! Mr Darvill still believed her claim and was making her an offer — an offer he would be compelled to retract the moment her papa disclosed the true state of her expectations! Ohh!

She tried to rise from the sofa but her lack of food over the past few days had weakened her more than she had thought. Her legs buckled under her and she fell in a faint at Lady Hartridge's feet.

Patricia was lying once more upon the sofa when she came round, with Lady Hartridge seated beside her. She tried to speak but Lady Hartridge placed a finger upon her lips.

'Do not try to speak, my dear. It has all been too much for you, I'm sure.' She patted her hand comfortingly. 'It shows your deep level of sensibility, my dear. Such a credit to you. Now, Kettering is making arrangements for you to be carried upstairs to your room and you must remain there for three more days at least. I blame myself for allowing you to rise from your sickbed too soon. This time I am determined you must stay there.'

Kettering returned with two footmen at that moment and Patricia felt too weak and ashamed to argue, but, in the quiet moments of the following day, when she was left alone to rest, she knew there was only one course open for her to follow. She couldn't face trying once more to apprise Lady Hartridge of the true state of affairs — she must leave London before Mr Darvill returned!

Determined now upon her course of action, she made herself eat all that was put before her in order to build up her strength, for she really had no idea how long it would take her to travel back to Lancashire. Not as long as it had taken her and Miss Quiggley to travel south, for they had travelled at a genteel pace and had stayed in a number of hostelries, but she doubted it could be done in a single day or even two days.

Why, Mr Darvill had been gone five days already and surely he would make the return journey as soon as he knew of her deception! He might even now be only a day away from his return, or even back already and about to denounce her! She must leave that very night . . . or, better still, in the early hours of the morning, for then she would have the day ahead of her to find a departure place for the coach and, hopefully, be able to board it at once and be on her way.

Her mind made up, Patricia began to ask for second-helpings, much to Mrs Wilkins's delight, and secreted as much food as she could into her small travelling bag. The bread would be stale and the cheese she had especially asked for, as it would be easy to transport, would no doubt go hard, but it would still be edible, and it was all she deserved after her display of such wickedness.

She would wear her warmest clothes, covered by her velvet cloak. The remainder of her beautiful gowns she would have to leave behind — and that would not matter, as she doubted if her mama and papa would allow her to step over their threshold in the foreseeable future!

She waited until Kitty had helped her to settle for the night and as soon as all was quiet, she slipped out of her bed and put on her stockings and dressed in her warm walking dress. Then she lay back under the covers for a while longer, knowing that the servants stayed up much longer than she and Lady Hartridge did.

At last, she decided she must leave. She checked that she had the remaining sovereigns from the money Uncle William had given to her in her reticule and her small quantity of bread, cheese and two apples in her small travelling bag. Then she tip-toed to the door and opened it silently. There was no sound to be heard, except some reverberating snores from Lady Hartridge's bedroom.

She had decided to leave through the front door, as she wasn't quite sure of the way down through the various rooms that made up the lower quarters and she hoped that whoever was first downstairs in the morning would assume they had simply forgotten to lock the door the previous night.

The sky was still quite dark and the cool air made her shiver as she hurried along the streets in the direction of central London. She had seen a stage-coach arriving in town when they had visited the Tower of London less than two weeks ago — was it really so short a time since she had last been so deliriously happy? — and so she headed in that direction.

Her legs were tired and she was feeling extremely shaky by the time she was in the area near to Covent Garden. Streaks of light were beginning to creep across the sky and the streets were gradually becoming alive with a side of life she had seen little of during her weeks in London. Road sweepers were brushing the streets of the previous day's trading and market traders were making their way to their places of work.

She asked a woman who was setting

up her flower stall where she might find a tavern where the stagecoach to the north might stop to pick up passengers and the woman pointed out a direction to her.

'Eh, what's a young lady like you doing out on the streets at this time o' day? Yer looks like yer needs a tot o' somefink, dearie!' the woman advised her.

Patricia had hoped that she didn't look too much out of place in her dark cloak and she pulled the hood further over her face. She agreed with the woman but knew that she didn't dare linger as she had no idea what time the first coach might leave. She was hoping it wasn't already too late and she hurried along the street where she had been directed. She had never been in these streets and she felt both disorientated and apprehensive.

The cobbled road was unswept and gutters were running with unthinkable detritus making the surrounding squalor and unwholesome smells more appealing.

How did these people live like this? It was much worse than anything she had seen in Liverpool, or had Mama and Papa shielded her from the worst of city living? Oh, the thought of her parents stabbed at her heart — how disappointed in her they would be! She was tempted to sink down on to the pavement and hope never to rise, but she was afraid to do so in this unkempt area.

A stitch in her side made her pause and she leaned against the wall of a building, taking a few deep breaths. As she straightened, a large-built man with a bundle under his arm lumbered past her on the other side of the street and vanished round the next corner. She prepared to continue on her way, when a young lad, better clothed than most of the population she had seen in this part of town, hurried in the man's wake, flattened himself against the wall at the corner and cautiously peered around it.

Patricia drew in her breath sharply. It was Jimmy, the street urchin she had persuaded Mr Darvill to employ! Even as the recognition came to her, the lad slipped around the corner out of sight.

'Jimmy!' Patricia called after him. What was he doing here? Hadn't Mr Darvill said Jimmy had become his shadow? Was Mr Darvill somewhere in the vicinity? Surely not! No, he must be following the man she had noticed — but why?

She was torn between pursuing her quest for the stage-coach and feeling concerned for Jimmy's welfare. He ought to be in Mr Darvill's stable-loft in Park Lane not here in this squalid part of town! Her concern for Jimmy won. She hurried across the road, narrowly missing being knocked aside by a man trundling a hand-cart and copied Jimmy's cautionary action at the street corner.

Jimmy was now about twenty yards away and the man out of sight. She hurried after Jimmy as fast as her weary legs would allow her. At least she didn't need to be as cautious as he. At every turn of the streets, Jimmy repeated his cautionary act before darting round the corner. Patricia had lost count of the number of twists and turns they had made — and suddenly lost sight of Jimmy also. He had followed the man into a narrow alley but neither was in sight. Patricia turned around. Where had they gone?

Two strong arms suddenly clamped around her and lifted her off her feet. She screamed and a smelly hand was clamped against her mouth and nose, cutting off the sound. She dropped her bag and tried to claw at the hand around her mouth but her gloves made the gesture ineffectual and merely resulted in a growling guffaw from her captor.

Patricia tried to call for help but only managed to make an inarticulate noise as her captor half-carried, half-dragged her through a narrow gateway into a small yard. She struggled to free herself but her efforts were in vain. She was dragged backwards into a dark hovel and unceremoniously dropped on to the flagged floor.

'Ouch!'

A sharp pain shot through her ankle and her head banged backwards on to the hard floor. She felt stunned and lay winded on the floor for a moment, until she felt a foot prodding her side. She scrabbled aside, trying to get away from the man who towered over her but her ankle shot with pain and the room was too small to get away far. Although there was a small aperture with a piece of sacking hanging over it that allowed a chink of grey light into the hovel, she could hardly see anything.

'Who are you? What do you want of me?' she demanded, trying to keep her voice steady, though the pain in her ankle brought her close to weeping.

'You again!' She sensed his recognition of her, as the man snarled, 'Flamin' busybody! That's wot yer are! Took me living, you did!' He reached down and grabbed her by an arm, yanking her partly upright. He swiftly grabbed her other arm and pulled them both behind her, wrapping some coarse rope around her wrists before dropping her to the floor again.

Patricia fell back again, her head banging against the floor.

'Wot yer gonna do with 'em, Jed?' a woman's voice whined.

'Shurrup, woman an' lemme think!'

A moan from the corner made Patricia raise herself up as far as she could and twist round to peer in that direction. 'Jimmy?'

'Cor, me 'ead hurts! What hit me?'

'Shurrup, I said!'

'What do you want of us?' Patricia asked again. 'People will be missing us. They'll come looking.'

'They won't look 'ere, will they — an' I'll be ready for 'em if they do!'

'It's the geezer wot 'ad the bear,' Jimmy hissed, shuffling over to her on his knees, his arms fastened behind him. ''E's nicked some gear from t'stables! I was following 'im!'

'Aye, wot 'ad a bear! That's right! 'Ad

but 'aven't got no more, cos of you, missy!' The man thrust his face down towards her, his breath reeking of stale alcohol. 'Now I 'as to find other ways to mek an 'onest livin'!'

'But Mr Darvill paid you for the bear and offered you a job!' Patricia protested.

'Wot? An' mek meself a laffin' stock wi' all me mates? Any roads, I'm a showman, not an odd job man! Now, shurrup. I'm thinkin'. I reckon that swell is plump in the pocket, ain't 'e?' He rubbed his hands together. ''E'll pay good blunt ter get yer back, but not 'im! I'd best dump 'im in t'river. The dead tell no tales!'

He bent down and hauled Jimmy to his feet but Jimmy wasn't going to be 'dumped' quietly.

'Gerroff me!' he yelled, kicking at the man's shins, causing the man to utter a foul oath and earning himself a hefty clap around his ear.

Patricia was horrified. 'You can't kill him!'

'Can't I, missy? You just watch!'

'But . . . ' Patricia thought quickly. 'But you'll be throwing away good money! Mr Darvill has . . . taken quite a liking to him. If he'll pay for me, he'll pay for Jimmy, too!'

'Yer wot? 'Im? Hmm? Mebbe yer right!' He dropped Jimmy down to the floor again. 'Tek good care of 'em, woman! I'm goin' out! I've got work to do!' — and the man stalked out, slamming the door behind him.

The woman settled herself on some sort of rough seating and was soon noisily drinking rum from a bottle, Jimmy shuffled back to be near Patricia.

'Oh, Jimmy! What are we to do?' she whispered. She wasn't sure Mr Darvill would be prepared to 'buy her back', though maybe Lady Hartridge would, if she were given the opportunity. But what if Mr Darvill was still away? Would this felon be prepared to wait?

'Don't worry, miss,' Jimmy whispered back. 'I've been in worse corners than this one. Me pals don't call me 'Lucky Jim' fer nothin'! Wait 'til the old biddy's dropped off an' I'll get us out o' 'ere in no time at all!'

His optimism was well-founded. The woman soon began to sing off-key snatches of tavern songs and when these petered out into no more than mumbled odd words, Jimmy got to work loosening the rope that bound his arms behind him.

''Is missus tied me up and didn't do it tight enough!' he whispered in between soft grunts. He was silent for a moment or two, then, 'There we are I'm free! Now, let me get at yours.'

He tried to undo the knots but the man had made a better job of fastening them, and the woman began to stir.

''Ere! Wot's goin' on?'

'Nothin'! 'Xcept there's rats!' Jimmy mumbled.

The woman laughed. 'There's plenty o' rats in t'river! Yer might be joinin' 'em!' she cackled and then dropped her chin again.

'Go without me!' Patricia urged Jimmy quietly. 'My ankle hurts anyway, so I can't run. Get help! Will you be able to find your way back?'

'Aye! I knows these streets like t'back o' me 'and. Yer sure yer want me to go?'

'Yes. It's our best chance . . . and he's less likely to kill me than you!'

'Right!'

The door was locked, barred from the outside. Jimmy climbed up to the small window and managed to wriggle through. He landed with a clatter on the other side but after a moment, Patricia could hear him struggling to his feet.

10

Gervais was in a quandary. He didn't know where to start. This was the last thing he had expected to find on his return to London! Miss Farrington was gone — and no-one knew where!

He had arrived at Lady Hartridge's residence at the unsocial hour of just before noon, simply because he couldn't bear to wait any longer after his return to London late the previous night, to find the whole house in an uproar. Lady Hartridge was distraught and alternating between pacing about the room in a state of agitation and sinking on to the sofa demanding her smelling salts, declaring time after time, 'But why should she run away when she is about to make the match of the Season? Where can she be? Why has she gone?'

Gervais had a very good idea as to why she had gone and he belatedly regretted leaving for Lancashire without speaking to Miss Farrington about it first. He knew he had acted that way because of Miss Farrington's reluctance to trust him with her 'problem', but she had been very close to telling him a couple of times and he could have helped her out. Hadn't he chosen not to do so in order to show her who was in control? To punish her a little . . . and then sweep her off her feet with his grand gesture of forgiveness?

But, instead, she had taken fright with the fear of being exposed as a deceiver! And hadn't he been just as guilty of deception? He had known from the start that her claim to be an heiress was made in a fit of pique after overhearing his arrogant claim that he was tired of being hunted for his fortune . . . and he had enjoyed 'foisting' her on to the gullible, materialistic pillars of Society, amusing himself at their expense . . . and at Miss Farrington's expense! He deserved her rejection of him!

He had driven back to his town house in Park Lane, his grim expression causing his staff to jump efficiently to his bidding and raise their eyebrows behind his back. Something had upset their master! Had he heard of that street-urchin's treachery? They didn't know . . . and no-one wanted to be the one to ask!

Gervais strode into his home, tossed his hat and driving gloves at a startled Wallis and disappeared straight into his library, where he paced the floor in as much agitation as Lady Hartridge had displayed. His heart contracted as he thought of how distressed Miss Farrington must have been to take such drastic action to avoid his return. She didn't deserve that! Why, she was as openly honest as an innocent child, which was what she was, and, he had to admit, it was that quality that had drawn him to her. But, where was she? What would she have been thinking? Where would she seek refuge?

There was only one answer — and

that was home! He must return there at once! He leaped up the stairway, heading for his bed chamber. No! Wait! There was something else to consider! How would she get there? She had no experience of travelling, but the transport she would head for would surely be the stage-coach. It would have to be! She wouldn't know any stopping places but, no doubt, she would expect to find one in town. Surely someone must have seen her?

That was it!

He would get all his men out on the streets and somehow they would track her down! If he discovered where she had boarded a coach, if she had boarded one, then it would be a simple matter to race after it and bring her back!

'My riding clothes!' he bellowed, ripping off his elegant necktie. 'Immediately!'

Clad in his riding gear and top boots, he strode out to the stables . . . to find his second uproar of the day. Jimmy was struggling with Bamber, who seemed to be trying to prevent him from running across the yard to the house.

'Just wait 'til t'master gets to 'ere of wot you done!' Bamber was shouting, striking the lad across his shoulders. 'After all 'e's done fer yer, yer steal from 'im!'

'No, I 'aven't! Let me get to 'im! 'E'll want to know where 'is lady is! Old Jed's got 'er!'

'Jed? Yer in cahoots with the old codger, that's wot I think!'

'Let him go, Bamber. Come here, Jimmy. What do you know about Miss Farrington's whereabouts?'

'Quick, Mr Darvill! There ain't no time to lose! Jed's got 'er. An' I don't trust him not to do 'er 'arm if 'e don't get some blunt off you!'

'Calm down, Jimmy, and start at the beginning. How do you know Jed has got Miss Farrington and what he intends to do with her?'

Jimmy excitedly recounted what he

knew from when he had seen Jed make off with some valuable articles from the stables. 'An' I followed 'im, see, to find out where 'e was tekin' the stuff be 'e pulled a fast one on me an' 'jumped' me . . . and then dragged in that lady who you be'n tekin' around town and trussed 'er up like a chicken and sed as 'ow 'e'd get some blunt from you if yer want to get 'er back. She sed as 'ow ye'd pay fer me an' all, but I weren't so sure about that so I got away! She's 'urt 'er ankle an' couldn't run, so she sed I'd to go an' get 'elp!'

'And where was Jed when you got away? Is he likely to be guarding Miss Farrington?'

''E left 'is missus watchin' us and sed 'e 'ad work to do. More 'n likely, 'e'll be sendin' someone 'ere to get the blunt off yer! Eh, up! I bet this is 'im! Hey, Limpy! Over 'ere! Wot you got fer us?'

A lad even smaller and scruffier than Jimmy had been peering round the large wooden gate that led from the back mews. At Jimmy's words, he reluctantly sidled forward, one leg dragging behind the other. He looked fearfully at the group of men who were gathered around Jimmy and then back towards the gate, clearly wondering if he ought to make a run for it whilst he could, but then he wouldn't get the promised 'copper' and so he edged nearer.

'Yer won't bang me up, will yer, mister? Only 'e sed as I'd ter say 'e wants a 'monkey' fer the gel an' five 'yellow boys' fer 'im.' He pointed at Jimmy. ''E sed as 'e 'ad yer banged up, Jimmy.'

'I was but I got away. Is that wot I'm worth? Five 'yellow boys'? Cor!'

Gervais smiled at Jimmy's delighted expression. The lad had probably never seen one guinea, let alone five.

'And where am I to take this 'monkey' and the 'yellow boys', lad?'

''E ses as 'e'll give yer a day to get it an' then I'll lead yer to 'im.'

'And where is he now?'

'Prob'bly back 'ome in Tot'ill Fields,

mister. 'E ses 'e'll be rich an' won't 'ave ter work again!'

'Did he indeed! He'll be on hard labour for the rest of his life when I catch up with him! Right, Bamber! Gather all the men together. We're going hunting! Oh, and I'd better take the town coach to convey Miss Farrington home. And you, Jimmy, may ride up front with me to show me the way.'

'Cor!' Jimmy's face beamed. 'Go an' get all t'lads, Limpy!' he instructed. 'These coves might need our 'elp!'

Limpy hurried straight off, eager for some excitement in his drab life and Jimmy waited impatiently while Bamber organised the harnessing of a pair of fine chestnuts to his master's town coach. Gervais instructed his grooms and stable boys to make their way towards Tothill Fields in as unobtrusive a manner as possible.

Cotham, his coachman, was chagrined to learn he was to travel inside the coach on the outward journey but

Gervais was too fired up with anxiety and a natural urge to be actively involved in rescuing his beloved to be persuaded otherwise by Cotham's woeful expression.

Some time later, everyone was assembled a couple of streets away from their destination. To Gervais's consternation, about a dozen or so urchins gathered around them, agog with excitement.

'Tell them to go away, Jimmy! It might turn out badly. I don't want anyone hurt unnecessarily.'

''S'all right, Mr Darvill. We're old 'ands at this. It's called 'divershon'ry tactics'!' Jimmy gravely assured him.

'Is it, by Jupiter! What do you have in mind?'

'We'll kick a ball o' rags over t'wall and climb over after it, mekin' a row. Old Jed'll come out to clear us off . . . an' you an' your lot can nab 'im!'

'I'm impressed, Jimmy. Lead on!'

It couldn't have run more smoothly had it been a proper military manoeuvre.

All happened as Jimmy had predicted. Gervais and two of his small band of men climbed silently over the wall first and pressed themselves against the wall on either side of the door. The smell of the place gagged his mouth and he couldn't bear that his 'dear love' should have to remain inside a moment longer than she needed to, but he wanted Jed out in the open.

He nodded to Jimmy, who had also climbed on to the wall, and the boys began to kick their ball of rags around in the narrow alley, making the usual level of noise such an activity would provoke. Suddenly the ball was tossed over the wall, followed by howls of dismay from the lads and cheers as the lads swarmed over the wall into the small yard. As they argued vociferously, Gervais could hear grunts of annoyance from inside and the sound of Jed lumbering towards the door snarling oaths. The sound of a heavy bar being lifted on the other side of the door made him glance across at Bamber.

Both were ready.

'Gerrout of 'ere!' Jed shouted as he appeared in the doorway. 'Gerrout, yer bunch o' scum!'

'Ya, ya! Come an' mek us!' Jimmy taunted, waggling his thumb on his nose.

'Eh? It's you, is it! It's the river for you, me lad!'

He angrily left the shelter of his hovel but had only taken two steps when Gervais tapped him on the shoulder.

'I think not, my friend!' he drawled quietly.

'Yer wot! Eh? Eh?' He glanced wildly around his yard. It was filled with what seemed to be a horde of urchins and four or five grown men. He recognised Gervais and made a move to dart back inside but Bamber, was blocking the way. He turned back with his fists up and aimed a wild blow at Gervais.

Gervais ducked and then went in with a punch of his own, well-schooled in the art of pugilism at 'Gentleman' John Jackson's famous saloon in Bond

Street. His first punch hit its mark and Jed was felled. Rubbing his knuckles, Gervais stepped over him and darted inside, almost reeling back from the terrible stench. A large roughly clad female made a vain attempt to deter his progress but he pushed past her. His eyes could hardly make out a thing in the dark interior but a cry of recognition from the corner drew him in that direction.

She was struggling to get to her feet and he was by her side in two strides, helping her to gain her footing.

'My love! My love! Are you unharmed?'

A sob sounded in her throat.

'Yes . . . Oh, I hoped you would come . . . even though . . . '

'Hush! Not now.' Gervais drew her close and realised her hands were bound behind her.

'A knife, woman!' he commanded over his shoulder.

''Ere you are, Mr Darvill!' Bamber spoke from behind him. ''Ere, let me.'

He swiftly cut through the rope and

Patricia immediately let her arms fall forwards. Gervais knew they would be painful after being bound for so long and he chafed them a little through the covering of her sleeves. Then, he swept her up into his arms and made for the door.

The afternoon light was bright and Patricia turned her head in towards Gervais's shoulder but a round of cheering caused her to lift it again.

'Oh! Have they all helped you to find me? Did Jimmy . . . ?'

'He did indeed . . . and these are some of his friends.'

'Put me down. I must thank them.'

She struggled to be released but Gervais held her firmly. 'You can thank them at some other time. I am taking you home. Jimmy, run and tell Cotham to bring the carriage as near as he is able! Make way, lads!'

He placed Patricia on the seat of his coach, leaning against the corner with her legs upon the seat, and seated himself by her to prevent the movement of the coach causing her to slip to the floor.

'Can I ride on top, Mr Darvill?' Jimmy piped up from the doorway.

'Aye. Put up the step and close the door, lad.'

Patricia anxiously plucked at her cloak. 'Which home?' she faltered, as the coach jolted into movement. 'I don't think Lady Hartridge will wish to receive me. And I am in a dreadful state. I am not fit to be taken anywhere!'

'Lady Hartridge is waiting anxiously for news of you. I suspect she will have the servants standing by with jugs of hot water and clean clothing for you. You have had a nasty scare and need some loving care and attention.'

Patricia gulped. 'I don't deserve any loving care. You . . . you must know by now that I am not an heiress. I didn't mean to deceive everyone and . . . and, more and more, it became too difficult to tell you.'

Gervais took hold of her hands and

stroked the pads of his thumbs along the backs of her fingers. 'I am as much to blame as you are, my love. You didn't deceive anyone, except maybe Jeremy . . . and I confess that I am to blame for that. I allowed him to believe your tale and didn't do anything to stop him spreading the tale.'

'You know? Then, why . . . ?'

Gervais raised his eyes to look into hers. He could see her bewilderment and hurt. He deserved to be banished from her side, but he hoped she wouldn't treat him so harshly. 'Like you, I meant no harm,' he admitted quietly. 'I was bored with Society and all the pushy mammas and their daughters. I thought to teach them a lesson, but it was arrogant of me to speak of my dissatisfaction as I did, and then to risk your reputation by encouraging Jeremy. I am truly sorry. Can you bring yourself to forgive me?'

Patricia was silent for a moment, then, 'I . . . I was enjoying all the attention I was receiving. It made me feel pretty and wanted. I suppose it was the sin of pride. And then you . . . you made me fall in love with you and I thought . . . Oh! Was Papa disgusted with me? Is Mama angry? I know she will be very disappointed that I have wasted my opportunity.'

'They aren't angry at all . . . or disappointed. In fact, they are rather proud of you and are longing to see you again. I have invited them to come down to London to be with you when you are presented at Court.'

'Pardon? Presented at court? But, but that is impossible now!' Her eyes narrowed. 'You didn't tell them, did you? They don't know how wicked I have been!'

It was Gervais' turn to look shame-faced. 'I had no intention of telling them of . . . of what you said on our first meeting. I went to ask your father for permission to pay court to you . . . and he very carefully asked me about all my credentials . . . and we got along so famously, that I couldn't bring myself to admit that I had deceived his daughter and run the risk of ruining her reputation. He would have had me horsewhipped and thrown out of his house . . . and justly so!'

Patricia's eyes danced at the thought of her very gentle father horsewhipping anyone, let alone Mr Darvill! And she was beginning to remember some of the sweet words she had heard Mr Darvill murmur during his rescue of her.

'Did I hear you call me your 'love'?' she asked softly, looking at him through lowered lashes. 'It seems you did, but maybe it was just because you felt sorry for me and wished to dispel my fear in that dreadful situation?'

Gervais smiled tenderly. 'I love you like I have never loved anyone else! I want to ask you to become my wife.'

'Really and truly?' she asked. 'For if you are still shamming, then tell me so immediately and I will still find it in my heart to forgive you, but if you let me dare hope . . . '

'Really and truly!' he echoed seriously. 'I was caught by my own game and by your very tender heart and your caring ways. And your papa gave me permission to ask for your hand, but not until the end of your Season, for he said you had so looked forward to a Season in London, he didn't want you to become a staid old married lady before you had enough memories of young men falling at your feet to remember for the rest of your life!'

'Papa said that? Now, you are funning me!'

'I think part of it might have been your mama's words or Emily's. She sends you her love, by the way. And so does Thomas. He was gratified to hear you had bloodied Jimmy's nose with one punch. So, my dearest, darling Miss Farrington, may I pay court to you, with the expectation of you agreeing to become my wife at the end of the Season? Can you learn to love me as much as I have come to love you?'

Patricia's eyes opened wide. 'Do you

really love me? Even now, when I must smell so dreadfully?'

'I love you to distraction! See, I will get on my knees and implore you to put me out of my misery!'

To Patricia's amusement, he did as he said. She laughed aloud. 'Then I know your love is real! And I love you already, almost from the start! I didn't dare hope that you returned my love.'

She sighed with happiness and her eyes took on a dreamy expression. 'I suppose, once we are married, I will be able to help those who are in need . . . I am thinking of Jimmy and his friends, and even that horrid man, Jed, because he only did what he did because he no longer has a bear to dance and earn money for him, you know.'

'Yes, I know,' Gervais agreed gravely, regaining his seat beside her. 'And you see before you a reformed character! I am already thinking that maybe we can set up a system where homeless boys are given the opportunity to have somewhere to live and to learn a trade?

Would that be a good idea, do you think?'

'Oh, Mr Darvill, that's . . . '

'Gervais.'

'Pardon?'

'You may call me Gervais.'

'Oh! Yes! Of course!' She tried it out. 'Gervais. Mmm, I shall like that. I was just about to say . . . '

Gervais leaned forward and cupped her dimpling chin between his thumb and first finger. 'My darling love!'

Patricia's lips parted in a surprised, 'Oh!' and Gervais claimed them with his.

THE END

FAITH FOR THE FUTURE
A CHANGE OF HEART
ILLUSIONS OF LOVE
A DIVIDED INHERITANCE
ELUSIVE LOVE

We do hope that you have enjoyed reading this large print book.

Did you know that all of our titles are available for purchase?

We publish a wide range of high quality large print books including:
Romances, Mysteries, Classics
General Fiction
Non Fiction and Westerns

Special interest titles available in large print are:
The Little Oxford Dictionary
Music Book, Song Book
Hymn Book, Service Book

Also available from us courtesy of Oxford University Press:
Young Readers' Dictionary
(large print edition)
Young Readers' Thesaurus
(large print edition)

For further information or a free brochure, please contact us at:
Ulverscroft Large Print Books Ltd.,
The Green, Bradgate Road, Anstey,
Leicester, LE7 7FU, England.
Tel: (00 44) **0116 236 4325**
Fax: (00 44) **0116 234 0205**

THE SANCTUARY

Cara Cooper

City lawyer Kimberley is forced to take over an animal sanctuary left to her in a will. The Sanctuary, a Victorian house overlooking the sea, draws Kimberley under its spell. The same cannot be said for her husband Scott, whose dedication to his work threatens their relationship. When Kimberley comes to the aid of handsome, brooding widower Zach Coen and his troubled daughter, she could possibly help them. But will she risk endangering her marriage in the process?

NO MORE ROMANCE

Joan Warde

After the car accident which killed her fiancé and badly injured her, Claire is travelling by train to stay with her, hitherto unknown, Aunt Mary at Forresters Haven. Hoping to avoid the pity she's encountered since the accident, she's infuriated when, on the train, she meets her distant cousin, Adam Forrester, with his patronising manner. However, her Aunt Mary is kind and understanding, there's new interests to occupy her, and there's Timothy ... but Claire wants no more romance ...